When I See You

When I See You
© 2006 by Melanie L. Wilber
Revised and Updated, 2015
All Rights Reserved

4

Dedication

For Silas, Kayla, and Karinne
May you see God

Taste and see that the LORD is good.

Oh, the joys of those who trust in him!

Psalm 34:8

Chapter One

Kerri Kirkwood secured the clasp on her silver heart earring and sighed. She felt more nervous today than she had anticipated. This Saturday in mid August had been circled on her calendar since she had been working as a camp counselor for the summer, but she didn't feel any more sure about what she wanted it to hold than she had when she had moved into her cabin at Camp Laughing Water two months ago.

She sat on her bed and spent a few minutes praying, something she had done all along regarding her relationship with Dylan Jacobsen. He was a great guy. She had enjoyed her time with him back home this spring during the closing months of her high school years, and she didn't feel she had made a mistake in allowing him access to a part of her heart she had been waiting a long time to open for someone. He was kind and sweet and someone she could talk to about anything. But was he the right guy for her—the one she was meant to be involved in a serious relationship with? She hadn't known then, and she didn't now.

I need to talk to Amber.

Tossing a few things she would need for the day into her backpack and zipping it closed, she slung the lightweight bag over her shoulder and left the cabin. Camp Laughing Water would be her summer home for two more weeks before she headed off to college. She was excited about the new path awaiting her. Her high school years had been good. She had a lot of friends from school and youth group she missed, but she knew her college years would bring new friendships and hopefully provide some direction for her future.

For a long time she thought she wanted to become an obstetrician like her dad. She enjoyed science and anything related to health and medicine, and she thought following in her dad's footsteps would be the perfect choice for her. But during the last year she had become unsure. She knew becoming a doctor would be a lot of work. Four years of college, plus another four years of med school, plus her years of residency. She would be close to thirty before she could have her own practice, and she wondered how marriage and family would fit into all of that.

Maybe she was meant to remain single, and being a busy doctor would fit perfectly into that kind of life, or maybe she could make it all work—marriage, career, family, ministry. She knew it was possible if that's what God had planned for her, but it would definitely take the right guy who would be supportive of her goals, and it would take God directing her every step of the way. It used to seem so simple, but now three weeks away from beginning the journey, it seemed complicated and scary.

Walking down the path toward the cabins at the bottom of the hill, Kerri hoped Amber would be there. Her twin brother's fiancée wasn't her only friend here at camp, but Amber was the one she knew would give her the best advice—not just good sounding words, but words of truth from her heart that seemed to beat right along with Jesus like no one else Kerri had ever known besides her brother. Kerri's heart filled with joy and peace every time she thought of Seth finding a beautiful and wonderful person to share his life with.

Two years ago she and Seth had made a pact to not date anyone until after high school unless the right person came along for either of them. When Seth had broken that to begin dating Amber when they were only sixteen, she knew Amber had to be special to get her brother's attention, especially since he had only known her for a week.

He met Amber here at camp two summers ago. At the end of the week on the way home, Seth told her about this girl named Amber, and he didn't stop talking about her for the two weeks that followed while their family was on a camping trip. He wrote her every day and when they returned home, he had some emails waiting from her, and at that point he was gone. Kerri had known by the look on his face and the words of one of the messages he let her read.

Kerri had printed out a copy of that email and kept it in her Bible as a reminder to pray for Seth and Amber. She wanted them to have a solid relationship that was honest and real and pure, and as far as she could tell, that's exactly what it had been. Now, two years later, they were engaged and planning to get married next summer.

She had also kept the email message because of what Amber had said about seeing Jesus in Seth's actions and attitudes. Seth had seen the same in Amber. And that was what she wanted: A guy who showed her Jesus: truth and love in everything. And she wanted to be the same for him. Someone with a pure heart who didn't just pretend to know God and talked about it, but someone who lived it. Lived the love. Lived the truth. Lived the joy of knowing God in a real, vibrant, life-changing way.

Dylan had passed that test. She had known him since the seventh grade, and they attended the same church in Portland. He had been shy back then, and she hadn't gotten to know him until about a year ago when he came home from a summer mission trip. He still had a quiet and shy side to him, but he had come out of his shell quite a bit, revealing aspects of his personality she really admired.

She hadn't seen him as a potential boyfriend, however, until he caught her one evening after youth group, asked if he could talk to her for a minute, and told her he wanted to spend some time with her in a courtship sort of way—not just asking her out on a date, but getting to know her in group situations and having her spend time with his family and vice-versa. His approach had appealed to her because she had been cautious about being alone with guys ever since someone had taken advantage of her in a secluded location when she was fourteen. She knew all guys weren't like that, but she also knew it was impossible to know what any guy would be like until she was in that situation, so she had avoided it with anyone she didn't know well enough to trust.

Her time with Dylan during the remaining months of her senior year had been enjoyable and not threatening in any way. She told him about her negative experience and that she hadn't kissed any guy since, so he had been open to taking things slow and not kissing her until they both felt they had something with the potential to last on a long-term basis: not necessarily marriage, but possibly, and Dylan had kept his word. He hadn't kissed her until three months later, and at the time she knew without a doubt in her mind she wanted him to.

It had been nice and made her realize she did have some strong feelings for him. For several weeks following that day she felt content and happy. In many ways their relationship remained the same as it had before and yet became deeper and took on a quality she had never experienced.

But as their senior year came to an end, she began to think about being separated from him during the summer while she was at camp and he was on a mission trip to Guatemala, and when they would be separated during the school year with her going to Lifegate Christian College in California and him remaining here in Oregon. She began to wonder if she wanted a long-distance relationship with a guy who was a better conversationalist face-to-face than over the phone. They hadn't communicated in other ways yet, but she didn't know if she wanted to go into her freshman year of college that way.

At the beginning of the summer she thought it would be better to end it rather than dragging something out that wasn't going to work. She figured if they missed each other enough, they could always get back together later, but if they tried to hang on, they might end up hurting each other. She had been honest with Dylan about how she felt, and they came up with a temporary plan she was happy with: Remain together over their summer of separation and get together today to talk about how they were both feeling, but giving each other the freedom to explore other relationships during the time they were apart.

Kerri hadn't met anyone this summer she felt strongly enough about to take that step away from Dylan. A few guys had asked, but she turned them down without any hint of resentment for her and Dylan's relationship. Mostly she felt grateful for the excuse, but she wasn't certain if that was because she didn't like those other guys, or if she didn't want to let go of Dylan.

Knocking on Amber's open door, she stepped inside the cabin and saw Amber packing a bag for their day-trip to Portland.

"Whoa! Look at you," Amber said, turning to face her and giving her a big smile.

Kerri had forgotten about her appearance. She had been thinking about what this day would hold, not how she had chosen to dress and fix her hair, but this was the most she had paid attention to those details all summer. She wasn't dressed up, but compared to her usual clothing of jeans or shorts and basic tops, and the ponytail she had been sporting all summer, she knew this was a definite upgrade.

"I'm so nervous," she said, deciding to be honest instead of acting like this wasn't any big deal.

"Why?" Amber asked, sounding genuinely interested in her reason.

"I don't know. I have a bad feeling, Amber."

"What kind of bad feeling?"

"Like he doesn't want it anymore."

"Why do you think that?"

She hesitated before sharing her honest feelings. Not because she didn't trust Amber, but because she wasn't sure of them until now.

"Because I finally think I do," she said, unable to hold back the tears. She had been guarding her heart all summer, not wanting to give in to the difficulty of being away from Dylan, but she missed him, and she knew it. She was really looking forward to seeing him today.

Amber held her until she stopped crying, and then Amber said something to give her peace for the moment. "God knows, Kerri. He's already got it all worked out. If Dylan isn't the guy for you, He's got a better plan. You've waited on Him, and He won't let you down."

She stepped back and gave Amber a small smile. "I knew you were the right person to talk to."

Amber smiled and then changed the subject. "Did you talk to Jessica in the last half-hour?"

Kerri smiled. She had forgotten about Jessica's decision to talk to Chad today and let him know how she felt about him, and she appreciated the diversion from her own frazzled emotions.

"Yes. She told me she's going to be bold and has you to thank. What did you do this time?"

"I told her."

"You did?" she said, knowing Amber meant she had told Jessica she knew Chad liked her, but she felt surprised Amber would do that. "Does my brother know this?"

"No," Amber said matter-of-factly as if she was tired of Seth's determination to let Chad and Jessica figure this out on their own. Not that she blamed her. Chad was shy and Jessica was clueless. Watching the two of them skirt around each other all summer had been both sweet and frustrating.

"But she asked," Amber defended herself, "practically anyway. It was close enough for me. And somehow by the end of this day I don't think Chad will mind."

"I think you're right about that. He was a basket-case all week—adorable, but a basket-case. Being that close to her all day, and sleeping under the same canopy of stars, and watching her pray with two girls by the fire last night had to be torture for him, wondering if it would ever be."

"And it's still up to them," she said. "Jessica could chicken-out, or Chad could be a complete jerk and say he has other plans. I'm staying out of it, but I just had to tell her. I couldn't stand it!"

Kerri laughed. Amber finished packing her bag, and they left the cabin, heading for the dining hall. They were early for the staff meeting, but others were there too. Kerri saw her friend Lauren and stepped over to say 'hi'. She hadn't had a chance to talk to her all morning.

They had become close friends over the summer. Their cabins had been side-by-side, and they usually hung out together on Saturdays. Lauren reminded her of Amber, only she didn't have a boyfriend and had never dated anyone. They were the same age and were both planning to go to Lifegate in three weeks, but Kerri thought Lauren was more mature than herself.

"How are you?" Kerri asked, giving her a hug. She knew Lauren's week had been difficult. She'd had a hard time connecting with the high school girls in her cabin. She had opportunities to share with them about the difference God could make in their lives, but Lauren didn't feel any of them were listening, so it had been draining for her.

"Okay," Lauren said. "I'm glad it's over. I know that's a terrible thing to say, but that's how I feel."

"You did what you could," she assured her, hearing Lauren break into quiet tears. "I was a total brat to my counselor one year, and I probably made her feel the same way as you, but I listened to what she said and saw the truth of it later, even though I couldn't have cared less at the time."

Lauren didn't say anything until she stepped back and dried her eyes. "Wow. You look nice. How are you doing?"

"Okay," she said. "I have no idea what this day is going to hold, but I think I'll be okay with whatever it does."

* * *

Adam Jennings entered the dining hall and scanned the room. His heart leapt when he spotted Kerri across the room talking to Lauren. As hard as he had tried to stop thinking about Kerri, after having more time with her during the last two days than he'd had all summer, she had been the first thought on his mind this morning, and seeing her now, appearing absolutely gorgeous, wasn't doing anything good for his vow to accept the reality she was in love with someone else.

He had run into that problem before: being attracted to a girl who already had a boyfriend. He'd let it go in the past. He wasn't into trying to break up relationships so he could have the girl instead, but he knew without a doubt in his mind if Kerri didn't have Dylan back home, he would have asked her out at some point this summer.

She absolutely captivated him. He liked everything about her. The last two days, while they had been on a rafting trip together with the adventure campers, had been like heaven and torture at the same time. He felt the same way now.

He hadn't had any definite plans to talk to her this morning, but when he saw Lauren step away, and Kerri didn't appear to be herself, he wandered over. On Thursday night after they set up camp along the river, he had gone for a walk and found her down by the water alone. She had ended up crying on his shoulder. He'd been a friend and listened, not giving her advice one way or the other. He kept his own wishes on the matter to himself and planned to do the same now, but he was drawn to her just the same.

"So today's the big day, huh?"

"This is it," she said, giving him a nervous smile.

"You can cry on my shoulder again tonight if it doesn't go like you hope," he teased her.

Kerri laughed. "I'm sorry, Adam. I'm a mess."

"He must be a special guy."

"What makes you say that?"

"Look at you. You look amazing."

Kerri laughed. "Compared to two days of rafting?"

"Compared to anything," he dared to say. She had a natural beauty that was there whether she was all fixed up or being a camp counselor. "He's a very fortunate guy, Kerri Kirkwood."

Kerri sighed. "Thanks, but I'm not sure I'm the right girl for him. I want to be, but I'm not sure that I am."

"Well, I know you're the right girl for somebody, and whoever he is, I'm sure you'll figure it out when the time is right."

Chapter Two

On the two-hour drive to Portland, Kerri felt better than she had all week, including this morning. She had been looking forward to today with a mixture of excitement and dread, but now that it was finally here and she could face reality instead of spinning all kinds of scenarios in her mind, she felt God's grace upholding her and talked freely with her brother about her current thoughts.

She was driving, and Seth was sitting in the front passenger seat because Amber had said she could use a nap. Amber was sleeping in the back, and Kerri told Seth what Amber had said to her this morning that made her feel better.

"That's why I'm with her," Seth teased. "It's all for you. Once I've got you married to the right guy, I'll let her go for a girl with more than a beautiful smile, a beautiful heart, and a knack for saying the right thing to my sister."

"Yeah right," she said. "The day you let her go is the day I disown you as my brother."

"She's right, you know," he said seriously. "She usually is."

Kerri gave him a sideways glance. "Did she tell you about Jessica?"

"Tell me what?"

Kerri laughed. "You'll have to ask her."

"I told her," they heard Amber say from the back seat.

Seth turned around. "Told her what?"

When Amber didn't reply, Kerri interrupted and asked Seth something. "Did you talk to Chad before we left?"

"No. I didn't see him."

"I didn't see Jessica either. I don't think either of them were at the meeting."

Seth glanced back at Amber once again. "All right, sweetheart. What did you do?"

"She sort of asked if you had ever said anything to me about Chad liking her, and I told her he did."

"*Sort of* asked you? What's that mean?"

"She was going to ask. I just helped her to say it."

Kerri laughed. If Seth had one weakness, it was Amber's ability to come across as sweet and innocent, even when she wasn't.

"You're in big trouble," he said. "When Chad asks who blabbed, I'm telling."

"He had plenty of opportunities this week according to Jess. I'm making no apologies."

***

Mandy Smith stepped out of the car and smelled the clean ocean air. Smiling at Matt who had opened the door for her, she received a sweet kiss and looked forward to receiving more before this day was over.

She loved being kissed and felt amazed Matthew Abramson wanted to do so. It had been three months since he had first kissed her. That had been on a beach too, and she couldn't think of a place she would rather spend a whole Saturday alone with him during their busy summer.

She had been working at Camp Cold Springs near Eugene, and he was at Camp Laughing Water about an hour away with her cousin Amber and Amber's boyfriend, Seth, who was also Matt's best friend. That's how she'd met him. She had gone on a weekend retreat with Amber in March. It was with Seth's youth group, and Matt had been there too. She liked him instantly. He was good-looking, a popular and vocal member of the youth group, and he had been sweet and nice whenever he talked to her. She thought it was only a crush and a guy like Matt would never see her as anything besides Amber's cousin. She thought she would never see him again after that weekend, but she was wrong.

She hadn't known it at the time, but Matt had been attracted to her too. Once Seth found out from Amber she was interested in him also, they set them up when she went to a concert with Amber and Seth's youth group a month later and then again when they'd gone to the beach in May. Matt knew about the dates in disguise, but she didn't. She couldn't figure out why he kept talking to her and sitting beside her, but she didn't do anything to try and discourage him. His presence had made her feel nervous and yet comfortable at the same time.

He had kissed her that day at the beach and they had been officially dating ever since, but she still felt that way with him. Being with Matt didn't get old. She was fine with sharing their time together with Amber and Seth and some others, but since everyone else had their own plans today, she welcomed the chance to have him all to herself on the one day of the week they had together.

Walking down to the beach from the parking area, they removed their flip-flops in the soft sand and stepped through the warm granules toward the mild waves rushing thunderously onto the shoreline. Matt took her hand and lifted her fingers to his lips, kissing them gently and then stopped to kiss her lips also.

"This is going to be a good day," he whispered.

She smiled at him.

"What do you want to do?" he asked.

"Besides this?"

"Yes. If all we do is kiss all day, I'm going to get myself in trouble."

She smiled and enjoyed the feeling of his lips on hers once again. She had never been kissed by anyone besides Matt, but she couldn't imagine anyone kissing her with more tenderness and genuine loving affection. She knew it wouldn't be wise to spend all day doing nothing else, but there was a part of her that wanted to take advantage of this time alone they had today. She enjoyed hanging out with other couples, but time alone with Matthew had been rare. She was more herself when it was just the two of them, and she knew he was more himself too.

"All right, enough of that," he said, speaking more firmly this time and taking a step away from her. "I'm melting like butter here, Amanda Smith, and it's barely past lunchtime."

She reached for his hand and stepped toward the ocean once again. "Let's walk for a little bit," she said, "and then you can take me shopping and buy me something."

He laughed, put his arm around her waist, and pulled her against his side as they continued walking toward the water. He was tall—over six feet, and she was barely over five, but she liked it that way. Whenever she was in his arms, she felt safe and secure. She didn't understand why he wanted her as his girlfriend, but she was learning to accept it.

She had been praying for a guy exactly like Matt for about five months before she started dating him, and God had answered in a major way. She had been cautiously optimistic, believing God could do such a thing, but also knowing He might have her wait a few years. But she hadn't had to wait long, and now that she was with Matt, she wanted to do everything she could to enjoy their relationship and make it meaningful and special. Something that would last. Something that was a benefit to both of them. Something like Amber had with Seth.

"You know what I'm looking forward to most today?" Matt said.

"What?"

"Having you all to myself."

She looked up at him and got chills from the tender tone in his voice. Matt was a social and popular person. He could talk above a crowd of people and command everyone's attention easily. Not in an annoying or obnoxious way, but an appealing one. Everyone liked him.

But he also had a quiet side, and she was one of the few who got to see it. And with no one around them today, she was going to get a good dose of the Matthew Abramson few did, and she was planning to enjoy every moment.

"I missed you this week," she said.

"And I missed you, Amanda. Only two more weeks and then we'll be seeing each other every day. Are you sure you want that? You might get tired of me."

"I don't think so," she said, stopping her stride as they reached the water's edge. She only had to smile at him to get what she wanted, and when he leaned down and kissed her tenderly, she told him exactly what she was thinking.

"I won't get tired of you, Matthew. I want to enjoy every second. I just hope you don't get tired of me."

"I can't imagine that, Amanda. I think you're stuck with me."

"I'm glad, Matthew. I hope you're my one and only."

Chapter Three

Blake Coleman took a deep breath and let it out slowly. Glancing over at Colleen in the seat beside him, he reached for her hand and held it loosely in his. She smiled at him, and he smiled back, but he wondered what she was thinking. She'd been quiet today. They had been on the road for an hour after stopping for lunch in Eugene, and they had another hour to go. Was she regretting her decision to spend the day with him?

"Are you okay?" he asked, trying not to let his insecure thoughts show but letting her know he was genuinely concerned. He had been pursuing this relationship with her for more than a month, and If she didn't want it, he didn't either; but he hoped she did because he had never felt this way about anyone.

"I'm fine," she said, giving him that smile he loved so much. It told him she was being honest, and hope returned to his doubtful heart.

She was so beautiful, and he loved being with her. He was hoping she would let him kiss her today, but he told himself to not get too set on that. Besides the fact in another three weeks he would be leaving for his senior year at Lifegate, and she would be remaining in

Portland to attend Bible college there, another factor had kept Colleen from letting him get too close thus far. Only a month before coming to Camp Laughing Water this summer to be a counselor, she had broken up with the guy she had been dating for a year and a half.

It had been a circumstantial breakup more than an emotional one. Her boyfriend was going to be gone on a mission trip this summer to China, and then he was planning to go live with his grandparents in Vietnam for a year and attend school there so he could learn the language better with the hopes of returning at a later time to do some mission work. Possibly as a doctor. Chris wasn't sure but had felt called for several years to take the love and message of Jesus Christ to that part of the world, and Colleen wasn't sure if she fit into that, so she had decided to let him go for now and see where God led them both in the coming year.

When Blake had first expressed an interest in her, Colleen told him she wasn't ready for another relationship, and Blake had respected her feelings. He felt content to be friends, and he hadn't made an effort to take things any further than the nice conversations they'd had on a couple of lazy Saturdays.

But then they'd gone to Silver Falls with a bunch of friends from camp, and she acted different with him than before. He learned a lot of things about her—personal things he didn't think she would share with just anybody, and she had smiled at him and given him looks that made his heart feel strange and share personal tidbits about himself he wasn't used to telling anyone he had known for a short time, especially a beautiful girl he normally would feel tongue-tied around.

Since then he hadn't been able to get her out of his mind. He thought about her at all hours of the day, and two weeks later he had been bold enough to ask her to spend a couple of days with him and his family at Sunriver on their extended break last month. He had been surprised when she said yes, and even more surprised at the really fun time they'd had. Not because he didn't expect her to be fun, but because he wasn't usually that social. He preferred a small band of close friends he knew well and had common interests with rather than meeting new people and trying new things.

They had a good mix of common interests and different ones. Last weekend they spent three hours together at the camp lake, sitting in a shady spot by the water and reading—something they both could spend all day doing, but then they had gone out for pizza and played miniature golf and video games the rest of the evening—something he hadn't done since he was twelve.

He smiled at the thought. It had been fun. Colleen had a serious nature, but she had been trying to be more carefree and childlike, and he knew he needed to do the same. Sometimes he got too caught up in the seriousness of life—his future plans and career and how he was going to live his life for God in the best possible way, but he often forgot God wanted him to enjoy his life in the process. Colleen was on that path to discovering the balance, and he was happy to watch and listen and allow her to teach him something about the lighter side of life.

"What are you thinking about?" she asked him. A favorite question of hers. It had been unnerving at first, and he hadn't known how to respond. But he had learned it was best to be honest.

"I'm thinking about you."

"And what are you thinking?"

"I'm looking forward to this day with you."

She smiled but didn't respond, so he prompted her.

"Are you looking forward to spending the day with me?"

"Yes," she said.

"Why?"

"Because I love being with you."

"You do?"

"Yes. Do you like being with me, Blake, or is it just better than being alone?"

He hadn't thought about it in those terms before, but he knew the answer. "I'm fine with being alone, Colleen. I'm not asking you to spend your Saturdays with me so I can be with someone, I'm asking so I can be with you."

She smiled at his words and laid her other fingers over his hand. Her light brown skin was smooth and soft. She had the most delicate looking hands he'd ever seen, and he loved seeing the silver band on her right ring-finger he had given her last week. She had been on crew staff instead of counseling, and they'd had a chance to go for a walk one evening. He gave her the ring because he wanted her to know he was serious about wanting this to go beyond the summer.

If she didn't want that, he would understand, but he didn't want her thinking this was a summer fling for him.

He hadn't dated anyone since his freshman year of college—intentionally. He'd been in a relationship that hadn't been good. The girl had been pushy and manipulative, and the whole experience had soured him on dating. It had been a huge distraction from his studies, and his grades had suffered. He had also been left with confused and guilty feelings—like he had done all the wrong things and hurt her terribly, but he had no idea why.

Looking back now, he knew it hadn't been him. He treated her fine and had done everything he could to try and make it a positive relationship, but she had wanted someone else. Someone who fit into her social circle and believed the whole world revolved around her.

One of the things he liked about Colleen was she allowed him to be himself. He didn't have to change for her or bend over backwards to please her. She liked him for who he was, and she accepted his friendship and presence easily. She didn't have to. She wanted to, and he wanted her to be exactly who she was also.

Continuing down the mountain highway toward their destination, he decided to live this day for whatever it held and enjoy his time with Colleen for whatever it was. In two weeks he might be saying good-bye to her and never see her again, but for today she was here, and she wanted to be. That was enough to bring an incredible feeling of joy to his heart, and he would hold on to the tiny strand of hope he would never have to say good-bye.

***

Kerri searched for Dylan's number on her phone with trembling hands. He was expecting her to call at this time, but she had no idea what to expect from him or what she wanted at this point. All morning she had been telling herself to wait and see, but now that the moment was here, she felt nervous about talking to him, more than she ever had before—even that first time she'd gone with his family to his sister's dance recital.

He had been the nervous one that night. She felt confident about herself, but he didn't, and she knew it. She spent most of the night trying to set him at ease she was enjoying herself, and she was. Dylan was an easy person to be around. Kind and sincere. He didn't have annoying habits or make her feel uncomfortable in any way. He'd been a guy she could trust, and that had been a big deal for her.

It had taken her some time to decide if she wanted to be in a relationship with him. Mainly because of the timing. He was planning to go to a Christian college near Portland, and she had applied to Lifegate in northern California. She kept their relationship low-key for about a month, then told him she wanted to just be friends because of the distance-thing they would eventually be encountering, but she made a serious effort to maintain the friendship they had gained.

And then out-of-the-blue she was walking with him on the beach on a youth group day-trip, and she decided she needed to take the plunge. Take a risk. Find out what it would be like to be kissed by an incredibly decent guy who adored her. That's what she had been waiting three years for, but when he finally came along, she had been scared to let it happen.

It had been an amazing first kiss, and she didn't regret anything. She never would. It hadn't been a mistake or a moment of fleeting pleasure. It had been a healing balm to her soul. Even now the thought made her smile.

She took a deep breath and waited for him to answer. She reminded herself of what Amber had said: God knew what this day would hold, and whatever it was, it would be in her and Dylan's best interests. Maybe not exactly what either of them thought they wanted, or maybe it would. Either way she knew they were seeking God's best for their lives, and she had to believe God would be faithful to guide them.

She heard Dylan's live voice greet her. "Hey, Kerri. Are you here?"

"Yes. We just got home."

"Any interest in seeing me today?"

"Yes. What did you have in mind?"

"How about if I come pick you up and we'll decide from there?"

"Okay. Now?"

"If that's okay."

"It's fine," she said. "It's good to hear your voice. I've missed you."

"I've missed you too, Kerri. I'll be there in ten minutes."

"Okay. See you."

Chapter Four

Adam checked his mailbox and took out the simple white envelope. Another letter from Mom and Dad. He opened it and scanned the words. Nothing too exciting; just the normal news. His dad's back was bothering him again. His mom was busy canning corn and beans and applesauce to fill their pantry for the winter. His younger brother had finished up his summer soccer league, and their team had taken second place.

"Hi, Adam," he heard a voice say behind him. He turned and saw Lauren had entered the room. She was the first person he'd seen in two hours. Everyone seemed to have scattered today, and he had begun to wonder if he was the only one who didn't have someplace to be or someone to be with.

"Hey, Angel," he said, calling her by her camp name. "I wasn't sure anyone else was still here."

"I know. I didn't hear about any group-thing today, but nobody's here. Where did everyone go?"

He shrugged. "Other than Seth and Kerri going home and Warner and Mariah going to the beach, I have no idea."

"Have you had lunch?" she asked, crossing the room to the kitchen area and opening the refrigerator.

"There's nothing in there," he said. "I already checked."

"Maybe there's some leftovers in the main kitchen. Do you want to go see?"

He felt like getting away from camp. Thinking about Kerri being reunited with Dylan today and being here mostly alone—It was depressing. "Let's go into town," he said. "I'm tired of camp food."

"Okay, sure," she said.

They stepped out of the staff lounge, and Lauren asked how he had enjoyed being with the adventure campers this week. He told her about the rafting part he had substitute-counseled for, keeping the details work-related rather than personal. Other than Amber, no one knew about his secret crush on Kerri, and he certainly wasn't going to tell one of her best friends.

There was no point anyway. He had been holding on to this tiny strand of hope ever since hearing from Amber that Kerri might not be continuing her relationship with Dylan, but if the way she talked about him this week and her appearance this morning was an indication of her intentions today, he knew it was time to give up the fantasy.

***

Kerri decided to wait outside for Dylan. She wanted their initial meeting to be semiprivate, and the front porch was the closest she could get to that in this house. Even in the ten minutes she waited, she was interrupted twice: once by her dad coming out to check the mail, and by Seth a minute later coming to check on her.

"You okay?" he asked, sitting down beside her.

"Yeah," she said. "I thought it might be better to meet him out here."

"Will you bring him in to say hello before you take off?"

"Yes. I'm sure I'm not the only one he'll want to see today."

"I think he would be just fine with that," he laughed, giving her a brief hug. "Have fun, okay?"

"Okay," she said. "Thanks, Seth. And I want details on Mike and Steph tonight, so pay close attention."

"Oh, I will," he said, referring to their older brother and his new girlfriend. "And you two always thought I would be the last one to fall in love. Ha! I'm engaged, you know."

"Yes, I know," she said, tossing a throw pillow at him. "Get out of here, Mr. Romance."

Seth stepped inside, and Kerri saw Dylan's car coming up the street. She took a deep breath and rose from the bench, deciding to meet him in the driveway, which she knew couldn't be seen from any windows or doors in the house because the garage hid it from view. She wasn't sure why she felt the need to do this in a private way. Normally she was very open with her family and felt free to share anything with them. But she felt more protective of her space today. Maybe because she felt insecure about what she wanted.

She didn't make it to his car by the time he killed the engine and hopped out. His appearance stopped her cold in her tracks. His light brown hair had been partially bleached and was much longer than normal, and his skin tone was considerably darker. The tan she could understand with him being in Central America for two months, but the hair? What was that about?

He came to her with a lopsided grin on his face. She remained frozen like a statue. Not only because of his altered appearance but her uncertain thoughts. Did she want this or not? She was out of time to decide.

Oh God, help!

He did the gracious thing, choosing to give her a heartfelt hug rather than a kiss. She could hug him equally whether he was a friend or her boyfriend, but she couldn't fake a kiss.

"You look amazing," he said, holding her close and setting her heart at ease for the moment.

"Thank you," she said. "What's with the hair?"

He laughed and stepped back, running his hand through the long strands. "It was a group thing," he said. "A bunch of us dyed our hair before we left. It's mostly grown out now, but I decided to wait to cut it so you could see, or I knew you'd never believe I had done it."

"You're right about that," she said. "But I'm proud of you. What's next? Belly-button ring? My name tattooed on your arm?"

He laughed. "I don't know. Maybe."

She smiled, enjoying this fresh side of him. Last summer he had returned from Mexico with a significantly altered personality. Apparently this summer had brought more changes, and she wasn't opposed to that. She liked Dylan for who he was, but she could embrace new things. Given her self-conscious thoughts all morning, she knew she was undergoing changes too. Graduating from high school and on the verge of the real world had made her more thoughtful about life.

Not feeling ready to kiss Dylan yet, she decided to have them go inside and explore that option later. "Everyone wants to say hi before we go," she said, taking his hand and leading him toward the front door.

He walked beside her in silence, and she felt awkward, as she feared she might. It was rare for her to feel at a loss for words around anyone, and she didn't like it.

Come on, Kerri. Say something!

He stopped her before they went inside, taking her free hand as she reached for the door. "Hey," he said, turning her to face him.

She looked up and saw his insecure hazel eyes. They hadn't been there thirty seconds ago, and she knew he sensed her uncertainty and had lost the confidence he arrived with. She waited for him to speak from his heart. He never did anything less.

But he didn't speak. He did the unexpected, lifting his fingers onto her cheek with a steady gaze in his eyes. He kissed her gently and added a dose of passion, taking her back to their first kiss on the beach. He took her breath away.

"Have you missed me, Kerri?" he whispered. "Even a little?"

She smiled, liking this spontaneous, take-charge side of him. "Yes. I've missed you, Dylan."

"Is there someone else you're going to tell me about today?"

"No."

"Really?"

"Yes."

"Can I kiss you again?"

"Yes."

He did and she melted into his affection. Dylan was a better kisser than she had ever imagined. He was insecure and conservative about a lot of things, but kissing released a confident, passionate side only she got to see.

"I missed you, Kerri," he said. "Very much."

***

Blake pulled the car off to the side of the road and saw the beautiful volcanic lake come into view. It was the perfect shade of blue on this clear summer day, and he hated to wake Colleen from her peaceful sleep, but he couldn't resist.

He reached out his hand to stroke her cheek and swept her dark hair away from her face. She stirred, and he waited for her to open her eyes.

"We're here," he said. "And it's beautiful."

Colleen had never seen Crater Lake in real life. She'd seen pictures, but her family had never come to the southern Oregon attraction since moving from Arizona three years ago. It was in his backyard practically—less than an hour away from his hometown, and his family had come here almost every summer.

But he'd never been as excited about it as he was today. He knew Colleen was going to love it, and he knew that would surprise her. Growing up in Arizona, Colleen wasn't easily impressed with natural wonders. She thought Oregon was beautiful with its lush green forests and mountain peaks, but the Grand Canyon was hard to beat in her book.

He covered her eyes so she would see the crystal clear, perfectly blue water for the first time with clear eyes, not fuzzy ones just waking up and adjusting to the bright sunlight. She tried to push his hand away, but he wouldn't budge.

"Close your eyes," he commanded. "No peeking until you can take in the full view all at once."

She obeyed and he got out of the car, went around to her side, and opened the passenger door. He reached for her hand and guided her out. "No peeking," he said once she was on her feet but too far away from the edge of the viewpoint to see over the guard-wall fully.

"I'm not!" she said, laughing and falling right into him when she tried to take a step and hit his foot instead.

"Ouch!" he said, catching her and keeping her from losing her balance. "That was my foot."

"Sorry," she laughed. "You're the one who told me to close my eyes. Can I open them now?"

"Not yet." He closed the door and kept his arm around her waist to guide her to the wide ledge overlooking the lake.

"Step up here," he instructed when they reached the sidewalk, and she did. He led her a few more paces forward and stepped behind her, wrapped his arms around her waist, and whispered over her shoulder.

"Okay, now."

He watched her eyes open and take in the view. He partly expected her to say, 'That's it?' or 'A two-hour drive for this?' But she didn't.

"Wow," she said. "You were right. The pictures don't do it justice. It's so blue. I don't think I've ever seen that shade of blue before."

He smiled, feeling satisfied with her reaction. "Was it worth it?" he asked.

She kept staring at the water for a moment and then surprised him by turning and bringing her face in alignment with his. She smiled and he realized how close she was. Closer than they'd ever been face-to-face.

"It's worth it," she said. "But you know what would make it even better?"

"What? If it was in the middle of the Grand Canyon and surrounded by flowering cactus?"

She laughed. "Well, maybe. But that's not what I was thinking."

"What are you thinking?" he asked, wondering if he should back away instead of invading her space. He hadn't intended for her to turn toward him while he was holding her so close.

"I'm thinking about letting you kiss me."

He stared at her, unable to fully process her words. "Are you?"

"Yes. If you want to."

He smiled at her choice of words. He wasn't sure he'd ever wanted anything more. She lifted her arms and draped her hands behind his neck.

"I wanted you to kiss me last weekend, but I was too scared."

"Scared of what?"

"Letting myself fall in love with you."

He felt like he was dreaming. "Are you afraid now?"

"No."

"Why?"

"Because I realized this morning I already am."

He didn't want to ask the question on his mind, but he had to. His feelings for her were too real to have this be a rebound relationship.

"What about Chris?" he asked as gently as possible. "Are you over him? I don't want to be stepping on territory that belongs to someone else, no matter how much I want to kiss you."

Her answer was peaceful, and he knew she had already given this a lot of thought. "I think I fell in love with the idea of him, and he was a good friend. I will never forget him or regret our time together, but you make me feel alive, Blake. I'm not here just to be with someone, I'm here to be with you. And we could be overlooking this beautiful lake or the Grand Canyon or a hay field for all I care right now, because all I see is you."

He closed his eyes and drew her close. Resting his cheek against her hair, he searched his heart. Was he with her just to be with someone? Had he brought her here because he was tired of coming alone, or was it about being with her?

"You make me feel alive too, Colleen," he said honestly. "I've never felt this way about anyone."

She didn't say anything else, and neither did he. Other people had invaded their space at the viewpoint area, and he didn't feel comfortable kissing her the way he wanted to with a bunch of people standing so close by.

"Come on," he said, taking her back to the car. "I know a better place."

He drove them up the road to the head of a trail he knew well and led her down the path toward a completely private location with a full view of the lake. She commented on how beautiful it was and snuggled into his side in a way she never had before. Her trusting smile and the way she was looking at him left no room for doubt she wanted to be kissed.

"It's been awhile since I've done this," he said, feeling his heart pounding. Sometimes he felt confident with her, and other times he felt like he must be a complete idiot to be thinking he could ever be with someone this beautiful and amazing.

"I think you'll do fine," she said.

She gave him the confidence to believe that. He closed his eyes and kissed her nervously, but he slowly relaxed and became more passionate about it. He got lost in her.

"Is this okay?" he asked.

She smiled. "It's very okay, Blake."

He kissed her more, thinking about the wonderful feeling of having her close and the way she was opening herself up to him. He felt the rest of the world fade away. Even the beautiful lake took a back seat to what was taking place in his heart.

Chapter Five

Mandy took the waffle cone from Matt's fingertips and thanked him. After walking around the small coastal town for the last forty-five minutes, ice cream was all he could afford. They would be eating dinner later, and he needed to get gas before they headed back.

She didn't mind. She was basically broke too, and she didn't need him to buy her things. His kisses and sweet words and friendship were more than enough to enjoy this day with him.

Sitting at a table outside the small shop, Mandy asked him something she had been wondering about. "Are you planning to get a job this fall?"

"Yes."

"Do you have to, or do you want to?"

"Both. I like working, and I can use the money. Me and Seth are planning to apply where Blake works, and he's pretty sure he can get us on there."

"Where at?"

"It's a pizza place in town. He makes good money there, especially when he does deliveries."

She didn't need to work unless she wanted extra spending money. Her school expenses were covered by a full-ride scholarship, compliments of four years of hard work and a perfect GPA. But she thought it might be a nice change of pace to work some, and she wondered if Amber was planning to get a job. Maybe they could work together too, like at a retail shop or an ice cream place like this.

Mandy didn't know what she wanted to do with her life career-wise. For the last couple of years she had thought mostly about becoming a teacher, but during the last six months of her senior year, she had become burned-out on school, and she wasn't looking forward to going to college.

She was looking forward to being away from home, living with Amber, and seeing Matt every day, but her drive to succeed in school had left her, and she didn't know if she could get it back. Part of her wanted to get a job and work instead, but that seemed like a waste when she had worked so hard for the past four years and had what every serious college student wanted—an education at a great school she didn't have to pay a dime for. She wished she could give it to someone else. She wished she could give it to Matt so he wouldn't have to work and could concentrate on school more.

Matt wasn't certain what he wanted to study either, but he was a good student—smart enough to do anything he set his mind to. She was too, but what did she want to do? She had no idea.

After a nice dinner that evening, they walked to the beach and settled themselves in the sand against a large piece of driftwood, talking, kissing, and just being together. They couldn't stay too late because Matt needed to take her back to her camp and then get to his own by midnight, but she'd had sufficient time with him today and enjoyed their remaining hour together.

"I don't know if I'm going to make it two weeks without seeing you," he said as they walked to the car for the drive back.

"I told you I'd skip my retreat next weekend."

"I don't want you to," he said. "I'm just saying I'm going to miss you."

This would be her last week of camp, and next Saturday she would be going camping with the staff of Camp Cold Springs, but Matt had two more weeks to go. "I'll miss you too," she said, stopping her stride and pulling him back to her.

He held her close and kissed her tenderly. "I fell in love with you this summer, Amanda. And I know you fell in love with me. Don't stop, okay?"

"Okay," she replied easily.

***

On the drive back to camp, Adam was surprised it was almost four o'clock and he had spent the whole afternoon with Lauren. He hadn't spent any time alone with a girl like this all summer, and he found himself wondering if she'd had as good of a time as he had. After having lunch, they had gone shopping because they both had a few things they needed to pick up, and they ended up wandering all over the store together. They were both on the lookout for stuff they needed to take to college. Lauren had bought a new backpack and a lamp for her desk, and he'd picked up miscellaneous supplies: paper, pens, spiral notebooks, and a new basketball.

He'd known all summer she was going to be at Lifegate this fall. Her brother Blake went there, and Blake had been the one to get him thinking about it last summer. He had been really excited when he discovered Seth, Amber, Kerri, and Jessica were going to be there too, along with Seth's friend Matt, whom he had become good friends with over the summer, and possibly Chad who hadn't made his final decision about going until a few weeks ago. He was going to be roommates with Seth, Matt, and Chad, and he knew God had certainly answered his prayers about having good friends to hang out with at school this fall.

He and Lauren had talked about school today, sharing their excitement and fears about going off to college, but they had talked about a lot of other things too: their respective summers of ministry as camp counselors, the difficult and triumphant times they'd had with their campers, and the many good times they both had with other staff members.

She was different away from camp. At camp she was quiet and focused on the ministry. She was there for that, not the social scene, and although she had usually been on their group excursions on Saturdays throughout the summer, she usually hung around with Kerri or her brother. She was never the center of attention, but she wasn't reclusive either. She went with the flow and never complained or was in a bad mood.

And she'd been the same today except she had been more talkative. He'd never felt an awkward moment like he didn't know what to say or how to act, but she didn't drive him crazy with meaningless chatter either. She was sweet and fun, and he liked her. How had he gone all summer without noticing her?

"What are you going to do with the rest of the day?" he asked, walking beside her to the main camp area from the parking lot.

"I need to do my laundry," she said.

"Me too," he replied. "I put some in before we left, and since no one was here today, it's probably still there waiting to be dried."

"I'll go get mine," she said as they reached the fork in the path. One way led to the cabin area and the other to the lake and staff lounge. "Maybe I'll see you there."

"I'll walk with you," he said, deciding he may as well. If they were the only ones here, which he assumed since the staff parking area was mostly deserted, they might as well enjoy one another's company. She smiled at him, and they turned toward the cabins.

"I'm glad we both got left behind today," he said. "I had a nice time with it just being the two of us. I mean, after being in a group all week, it's nice to have a relaxing day, but doing laundry all alone would have been depressing."

"Yeah, I know. I'm used to hanging out with Kerri on Saturdays. I felt lost after she left."

"You two got to be good friends this summer."

"Yeah, we did. She's so different from me, but somehow we hit it off during training week and then our cabins were next to each other all summer. I think she needed someone to talk to—about Dylan and

49

everything. I guess she thought I was a good listener."

"You are," he said. "I'm not usually this talkative."

"Except with Kerri?"

Her question surprised him. "What do you mean?"

"You talked to her a lot this summer."

"I already knew her from last year. I meant people I don't really know, like you."

"You like her, don't you?"

He didn't respond.

"I don't blame you," she said. "She's beautiful and the kindest person I've ever met."

He tried to remain innocent. "What makes you say that? Did she talk about me? I mean, does she think I like her or something?"

"No. I can see it."

"See what?"

She smiled at him and laughed. "I can tell you the name of every guy here who wishes Kerri didn't have a boyfriend back home. Don't deny it, Adam. It's okay."

He let down his guard. What did it matter anyway? "I was probably more obsessed than I should have been. I did the same thing last summer with someone else I knew I couldn't have. Why do I do that?"

She laughed. "Who?"

"Amber."

She laughed again and let out a strange groan.

"What's that for?"

"Can you keep a secret?"

"Sure."

"I'm serious, Adam. I haven't told anybody this. Not even Kerri. If it gets out, I'll know it was you."

They stopped walking when they reached the trail he couldn't go down with her, and he glanced around. It was a wooded area full of heavy brush, and he knew someone could be close enough to hear them talking without them seeing anyone.

"You'd better whisper it to me, then," he said. "I'm not taking any chances around here."

She smiled and stepped closer to whisper her secret in his ear. "No one, Adam. I mean it."

"I won't," he said. "I promise."

"I've had a huge crush on Seth all summer."

He laughed.

"I couldn't help it. He's so cute and nice and everything!"

"Oh, so that's why you've been Kerri's friend. It's actually a secret ploy to—"

"Shh!" she said, laughing and putting her hand over his mouth. "That's not why, and not a word. You promised."

He pulled her hand away from his face, but he didn't let go. "I promise," he said. "Your secret is safe with me, Angel."

"I'm not seriously after him, but that's the kind of guy I'm looking for. Maybe that's the way it is for you too. Kerri isn't the one for you, but someone like her is."

He supposed that was true, although Amber and Kerri were very different. They were similar in some ways. They were both kind and fun and had great smiles, something that he found very attractive in a girl. But personality-wise, Lauren was a lot more like Amber.

She turned away to go to her cabin, and he waited there until she returned. She was carrying two small baskets, one full of light clothing and one of darks, and he offered to carry one of them for her to the laundry center in the basement of the staff lounge. He was right about his clothes still being in the washer he had put them in. After moving them to one of the dryers, he sat on the counter and waited for her to finish putting her two loads in, and then she came to join him.

They talked like they had been all afternoon. She shared about her difficult week and her hopes next week would go more smoothly. He told her his first week of counseling had been challenging because some boys couldn't seem to follow any of the rules, and that had made him dread the rest of the summer, but then all of his other weeks had been fine.

"Thanks," she said. "That makes me feel better. I've heard high school campers are supposed to be the most fun, but that wasn't my experience."

"Next week will be totally different," he said. "Sometimes God gives us a bit of a challenge to remind us we're supposed to be trusting Him, not our own abilities. But He knows when we've had enough. Trust Him, Angel. It'll be all right."

She smiled, and he was reminded of his earlier thoughts. Lauren had been here all summer, and he'd spent every Saturday with her in a group setting. Why had he just now noticed how much he enjoyed being around her and how easy she was to talk to?

"So what exactly appeals to you about Seth?" he asked. "I mean, what's your idea of the ideal guy?"

She laughed. "I don't know."

"Oh, come on. Yes, you do."

"He doesn't ask nosy questions, and he knows how to separate his laundry."

"Oh? Have you been down here doing laundry with Seth? Do I need to inform Amber of this, Miss Angel?"

"No. I can't believe I told you that."

"Maybe Seth doesn't know how to sort his laundry either. Maybe that's why he's dating Amber."

She laughed. "How about you? What do you like about Amber and Kerri?"

"They're honest and caring. Close to God."

"Beautiful," Lauren added. "It's okay. You can say it."

"Beautiful," he admitted. "Great smiles. Happy and fun. I don't know, they're just the kind of girls I can stand to be around for more than ten minutes."

Lauren smiled, and Adam once again realized all of those things were true of her.

"Now the thing I need to do is find a girl like that who isn't already taken."

"That would be a good idea."

Adam didn't consider himself to be spontaneous. He usually thought about something seriously before taking action. But the truth was he'd been thinking too much this summer about a girl he couldn't have and ignoring girls like Lauren who didn't already have boyfriends but were beautiful, honest, caring and he could have a good time with.

"So, are you seeing anyone?" he asked.

"Shut up," she said, pushing him away and laughing. She hopped off the counter to go take her clothes out of the washer and stick them in an open dryer. He watched her as she took out her whites first, carried them to the dryer beside his, put them in and then opened the adjacent one to use for her dark clothing. It already had laundry in it, so she took out someone else's dry clothes and set them on the counter beside him, all the while avoiding his steady gaze. She was really beautiful, he realized. She didn't have the kind of look he immediately took notice of when he saw a girl, but she was beautiful in her own way.

Her eyes were large and expressive. Her skin smooth, and her hair simple, but a wonderful shade of strawberry blonde. And although she had been open and real with him all day, he could see he'd made her uncomfortable, and he wanted to take that away. He wanted her to feel free to be herself and for her to know he found her attractive for exactly who she was—inside and out.

While she went to get her jeans and other dark clothes out of the washer to put them into the space she had cleared, he got down from the counter and began folding the laundry she had set on the counter beside him. It wasn't his, but he often put laundry in early in the day and returned that evening to find others had dried and folded it for him, so he always tried to pass that act of kindness on if he had extra time.

When Lauren came to help him, he didn't say anything for a minute, not because he didn't know what he wanted to say, but because he wanted to wait for the right moment. The door behind them opened before they finished with the pile, and Adam turned to see Chad enter the room.

"Hey, you're folding my laundry," he said, coming over to thank them and say he could do the rest.

"Where did you disappear to today, man?" Adam asked him. "You didn't go rock-climbing without me, did you?"

"No," he said. "I had something else to do. Where is everybody? You're the first two I've seen, and the parking lot is empty."

"I have no idea. I guess everyone had someplace to be today."

"I'm going back to my cabin," Lauren said, heading for the door and trying to escape. His heart smiled. She was falling for him too but was afraid of it. He didn't know how he knew that, but he did.

He allowed her to go out the door, but as soon as she did, he patted Chad on the back and said, "See you later, man. I've got something I need to do."

He didn't have to go far to catch up with her. She was walking down the trail toward the dining hall and the cabins beyond that, obviously not expecting him to come after her. He jogged casually up to her side and didn't say anything. When she looked at him, he smiled and said in a soft voice, "I had a really great time with you today, Lauren."

She kept walking.

"I'd like to spend this evening with you too, unless you have something better to do."

"What did you have in mind?" she asked.

"We could go into town, get some dinner, maybe a movie?"

"We just got back," she said.

"Are you turning me down?"

"I'm not that hungry yet. How about if we hang around here long enough for our laundry to dry so I don't end up folding clothes at midnight."

"Fine with me," he said. "What are you going to do for the next hour?"

"I don't know. What are you going to do?"

"Whatever you're doing, unless of course you're going to your cabin. I can't go there."

"I suppose I could do something else."

"Like go for a walk with me?" he asked. "I know I'm not Seth, but—"

That got her to smile again, and they both laughed.

"Okay," she said.

Chapter Six

Blake took Colleen to the Crater Lake Lodge for dinner. It was a little pricey, but with the fantastic afternoon he'd had, he didn't care about anything except making Colleen feel special, and this would say it better than the many roadside diners or fast-food stops on the way back to camp.

"Blake, this is too expensive," she whispered loudly after taking a moment to scan the menu. "We're not eating here!"

He smiled and took a sip of his water. "Yes, we are. Get whatever you want."

"Can you afford this?" she asked bluntly. "You're a college student who's been working a volunteer job all summer. This isn't going to be tuition money you're spending on me, is it?"

"If it was, it would be worth it."

She smiled. "I already like you. You don't have to impress me."

He reached across the table and took her hand. "I didn't bring you here to impress you. I brought you here because it's a nice place, and I want to have a special dinner with you. Do you know how long I've been dreaming of having dinner with a beautiful girl here?"

"I'm the first?"

"You're the first," he said. "And you're having dinner with a guy who's been working a steady part-time job for the last two years without a girl to spend any of that money on. I'm fine. I promise."

"You don't use that money for school?"

"A little, but not all. It's mostly for me to have spending money, but I eat on campus or at the pizza place most of the time, and while a lot of my friends are going out on the weekends, I'm either working or studying."

"Are you going to school on a scholarship, or are your parents paying for it?"

"Both. Scholarships and grants pay for about eighty percent, and they pay the rest."

"So why do you work so much?"

"I like it. It's a good job. It's owned by a Christian family, so it's a good work environment, but they hire kids from town too, so it's a good ministry opportunity. And it keeps me from overachieving in my classes."

"And that's a good thing?"

"Yes. It keeps me balanced."

She smiled, and he asked what that was for.

"That's why God gave me a friend like Amber. She reminds me to smell the flowers."

He brought her fingers to his lips and kissed them. "And you've been worried about not having her around?"

"Yes, a little," she said.

He released her hand and turned his eyes back to his menu. "Okay, then it's time for me to step in and take over. Order whatever you want and enjoy this evening with me, okay?"

He glanced over the top of his menu for her response.

"Okay."

Once he had decided what he wanted, he laid his menu aside and recalled the amazing afternoon he'd had with Colleen. After being cautious with him for the past month, she hadn't held back today. They had gone for a hike, stopping at various viewpoints around the lake, and he'd held her hand, held her gently against him, and kissed her many times. And unless she was really good at faking affection, he knew she had enjoyed it as much as he did.

On the drive back to camp after dinner, they talked like they had been all day but got quiet during the last hour. When they stopped in town to get gas before heading up the mountain, he asked if she was all right, and she said she was fine.

"Can I ask you something?" he said.

"Yes."

"You won't be mad?"

She smiled. "Hard to say since I don't know what it is."

He decided to take a chance. He needed to know if she wanted this before they went into another busy week of camp. "Were you kissing me today?"

She smiled. "You didn't notice?"

"Yes, I noticed."

"You mean, was I kissing you in my heart or someone else?"

"Yes."

She reached out and touched his cheek and leaned toward him, giving him a sweet and tender kiss. "I'm kissing you, Blake. And I've never enjoyed anything more."

***

Adam asked Lauren out for pizza after they had gone for a walk and finished their laundry, and she accepted the invitation. He took a few minutes to fix himself up after taking his clean clothes to his cabin, changing into fresh jeans, a nice shirt, and touching up his short blond hair in the bathroom.

Meeting her by the lake, he saw she had changed from the shorts and t-shirt she had been wearing all day into jeans and one of her trademark "Angel" knit tops. This one was dark blue with lighter blue lettering. She had taken out her ponytail, leaving her shoulder-length hair loose. He thought she looked nice but not any different than she had all summer, and he was amazed he suddenly saw her in a new way.

"So why did you choose the name Angel?" he asked as they walked toward the parking area.

"My middle name is Angela." She laughed at herself. "Real original, huh?"

"I like it," he said. "It suits you."

"Thanks," she said. "What's your middle name?"

"Randall. It's a family name. My grandpa's name is Randall, and that's my dad's name too. They spared me and made it my middle name."

"I don't know," she said, looking him over from head to toe. "You could be a Randy. It would work for you."

He smiled. "Thanks, but I think I'll stick with Adam."

They were both silent for a minute until they reached the truck. He opened the passenger door for her, but before she got inside, she said something.

"You know how I told you about having a crush on Seth all summer?"

"Yes."

"I have another confession to make."

"Oh yeah?" he said, liking this honesty and trust they were building with one another. "Another secret you're willing to share with me?"

"Yes," she said, appearing nervous but going ahead with it. "I knew I couldn't have Seth, but there's another guy I've seen in the same way who doesn't have a girlfriend, and I've been trying to figure out how to get his attention."

"Is this a way of telling me you'd rather be friends?"

"No," she smiled. "It's you, Adam. I've been dreaming of you asking me out all summer."

He was speechless. He thought he'd made a great discovery today and taken her by surprise, but in reality she had been watching him this whole time?

"You've never acted like it."

"I know. I'm really bad at stuff like that."

He didn't know what it was, but Lauren was making his heart do back-flips, and Amber and Kerri and all the other girls he had liked during the past couple of years seemed so dim in comparison. Lauren may have been hiding in the shadows all summer, but standing here before him with a whole evening stretched out before them, she looked absolutely radiant.

"Have I mentioned I'm an idiot?" he said, reaching for her hand and giving it a gentle squeeze. He would kiss her right now if it wasn't against camp rules. "I'm sorry I've been obsessed with Kerri and didn't notice the beautiful girl standing right beside her."

"You don't have to apologize for noticing girls like Kerri over me, Adam. I know I'm not—"

He stepped forward and stood as close as possible without their bodies actually touching. He took her other hand and waited for her to look up at him. When she did, he stated an observation he'd made earlier.

"You don't wear any makeup, do you?"

"No," she said.

"You're beautiful without it. I mean that, Lauren. This is the first day of the summer I've taken a good look at you, and I like what I see. But even more, I'm attracted to your heart. I have noticed that about you many times this summer without thinking about it. You're kind and you're generous and you're a good friend. And I hope you can forgive me for not paying more attention, because I really would like to get to know you better."

She responded softly. "If we weren't going to the same college together in three weeks, I might not, but since we are, I suppose I can overlook it."

He stepped back and smiled, and she got into the truck. He felt nervous as they drove into town, wondering what he had started, but the rest of the evening was as enjoyable as the hours since she had invaded his world before lunchtime. They talked nonstop, and he learned a lot about her. He tried to be open and honest with her in return. He often felt insecure around girls, but he didn't feel that way with Lauren. He could tell her anything.

One of the things he shared was his concern for his family. His mom and dad had always been stable and consistent. They were good parents to him and his two younger siblings, active in their church, and seemed to have a good marriage. But last year his dad had back surgery, was off work for two months, and they'd struggled some financially. Since then his dad had been different, using his back as an excuse to pull out of a lot of things at church and not attending consistently anymore.

His parents had argued more in the last year than he'd ever heard before, and in addition to the financial strains they had, his younger sister had become somewhat rebellious, and they yelled at her a lot too.

"I feel like I'm living in a different house or something. It's really weird, and on the one hand I'm anxious to head off to college and get away from it, and on the other I'm wondering if they can afford it or if I'll be causing them more problems."

"It sounds to me like you're the least of their problems, Adam."

"What do you mean?"

"Your dad's back, fighting about money, your rebellious sister: those are problems. A teenage son who spends his summer working at a youth camp, respects his parents, and is going to a great college?

I'd say you're one of their greatest blessings right now. I'm sure they're very proud of you."

They were still at the pizza place, sitting in a corner booth after they had finished eating an hour ago. And in that moment he knew without a doubt in his mind he needed Lauren in his life. She wasn't just beautiful to admire from afar, she was touching his heart in a way Kerri and Amber and no other girl ever had. And he didn't want her to stop.

Chapter Seven

Kerri listened to Dylan's stories about his time in Guatemala for much of the afternoon, and she enjoyed hearing about his great experience and all God had taught him. But as the afternoon wore on, she began to get the feeling there was something he wasn't telling her. Several times he mentioned a certain girl. Her name was Janelle, and she had either been one of the primary student leaders, or Dylan had spent more time with her than the average person on their team.

Dylan had gone to Guatemala with a youth mission organization that took students from all over the United States. He mentioned where several of the others were from. His best friend on the trip, Nathan, was from Florida, and another guy was from Texas. He hadn't mentioned where Janelle lived, so when he mentioned her again, she asked.

"Seattle," he answered without having to think about it.

Kerri smiled. All afternoon she had been more than happy to be with Dylan and go back to camp today with the reality she was his girlfriend, and she had no reason or desire to change that. But she wanted to make sure Dylan felt the same way.

"It sounds like you spent a lot of time with her," she said, not trying to accuse him of anything but stating a fact. "Is that how it worked out, or did you like her?"

They were walking through Waterfront Park along the Willamette River in downtown Portland. Dylan kept his eyes straight ahead and answered. "She knew I had a girlfriend. We were just friends."

Kerri laughed. "That's not what I asked."

He glanced at her but didn't respond.

"Dylan," she said, stopping her stride and waiting for him to do the same. He turned back and faced her, and she continued. "Be straight with me. If you hadn't had a girlfriend back home, do you think something might have happened? Would you have wanted it to?"

"Why are you asking me this?"

"Because I care about you, and I want you to be with the right girl. If that's me, I'm happy to be your girlfriend. I missed you, and I'm willing to give a long-distance relationship a try, but to be honest, I'm not in love with you yet. Maybe because it's going to take time, or maybe because I'm not the girl you're meant to love."

"What are you saying?"

"I'm asking you a question, and I want an honest answer."

He stepped forward and took her into his arms, giving her a warm hug she accepted easily. Dylan always made her feel safe and protected.

"I hate this, Kerri," he said, sounding emotional.

"Hate what?"

"Not knowing what I want and trying to figure it out."

She repeated her question but phrased it differently. "Have you been thinking about Janelle since you got back?"

He sighed and released her. "Yes."

"And what have you been thinking?"

He didn't answer immediately, and she waited. She could tell it took every ounce of strength he had to speak the words.

"I wanted to wait and see what happened with us. If you were looking elsewhere, and we said good-bye to each other today, then I planned to call her and let her know."

"And you told her that, before you said good-bye to her last weekend?"

"Yes."

Kerri felt a twinge of sadness. She adored Dylan, and saying good-bye to him would not be easy. He was the first guy she had opened a private part of her heart to, and the only guy she had kissed in a special way and had begun to care for. But she couldn't hang on to him if he was meant to be with someone else.

"Dylan, don't do this. Don't pretend to have feelings for me you don't have."

"I'm not pretending, Kerri. I care about you. I missed you. I wanted to see you today, and when you told me no one else had captured your heart this summer, I was happy to hear that."

"But you're still thinking about Janelle? Even now, after spending six hours with me?"

He didn't respond.

"It's okay, Dylan," she said, stepping forward and giving *him* a hug. "It's okay."

He started crying, and she couldn't believe she was going to let this incredibly decent, caring, and special guy walk out of her life, but she also knew she couldn't do otherwise. He wouldn't have told her about Janelle if he hadn't developed some strong feelings for her and wanted to see her again. And she wasn't going to stand in the way.

"I feel awful, Kerri," he said.

She stepped back and looked into his face. "Why? We both agreed it was okay if we met other people."

"I know, but I never expected it to be me. I didn't mean for this to happen."

"I know you didn't, Dylan. But it's okay. Really. You're the one crying, not me."

She laughed and got him to do the same.

"I know," he said, "but I'm the one who initiated all of this. I pursued you—twice. I got you to go out with me when you weren't certain you wanted to, and after you tried to end things in March, I kept hanging around until you finally gave in to me at the beach, and then—"

"Whoa, wait a minute, Dylan. We agreed to be friends, and you didn't talk me into anything on the beach that day. I wanted you to kiss me, and I have no regrets. I have no regrets about anything. If I knew this was going to happen, I would have done everything the same."

"You would?"

"Yes. You have been an incredibly special part of my life. I love you, Dylan, and I want you to be happy—with me, or with someone else."

***

When Seth saw Dylan's car pull into the driveway at seven o'clock and Dylan didn't get out of the car to walk Kerri to the front door, he had a feeling his sister had ended things with Dylan today. He knew if it was him driving his girl home an hour earlier than necessary and he wasn't going to be seeing Amber for another two weeks, he wouldn't be content with a quick good-bye kiss in the car.

His sister spotted him and Amber sitting on the porch as she came up the walk, and she gave them a sad sort of smile. "Hey guys," she said. "Whatch'ya doin' out here?"

"I was reading Amber a little poem I wrote for her," he said, getting up to give his sister a hug.

She held on to him for a moment. "I let him go," she said without him having to ask. "He met someone else."

Seth stepped back and looked into her eyes. "How do you feel about that?"

"I'm okay," she said in a way he knew she meant her words, but she was a little sad too.

"Feel like talking about it? Or would you prefer we left you alone?"

She sat in his place on the bench, and Amber gave her a hug. Kerri told them what her afternoon had been like, and they all laughed when she said Dylan was the one who ended up crying.

"I'll miss him. I'm not denying that. I'm sad to let him go, but at the same time I'm extremely happy for him. We all know Dylan isn't the type of guy to fall for a girl unless he's having major feelings for her, and I

69

could tell that when he told me about her. I sort of feel like she's one of my friends or something, and I would definitely wish a guy like Dylan on any of my friends."

She rose from the bench and said she needed to go inside to use the bathroom. Seth asked if she wanted to head back to camp now or wait another hour like they had originally planned. She said now was fine, and they decided that's what they would do. Kerri went inside, and Seth sat beside Amber.

"Do you think she's okay?" Amber asked him.

"Yes," he said. "But I'm not sure I am."

Amber laughed. He had told her many times how much he wanted Kerri to remain with Dylan. He trusted Dylan with his sister's body and heart, and he had peace whenever he knew they were spending time together, knowing Dylan would never try to take advantage of her.

"You keep praying," she said. "God has another Dylan out there for her."

"You pray too, okay?"

"I've been praying since I heard about what happened to her when she was fourteen, and if she was looking for a good guy before, she'll really be looking now. She won't settle for anything less than the way Dylan treated her. Girls don't forget guys like that."

Chapter Eight

On the drive back to camp, Kerri rode in the back seat by herself, and she did a lot of thinking. She had been honest with Dylan and herself today, and she felt good about the way things had turned out. Heading off to college without the complication of a relationship made her feel a lot better about going.

She wanted to enjoy this time in her life. New places. New people. New friends. Looking toward the future and finding the path God had for her. She needed that right now. She would meet the right guy for her at the right time, she felt confident of that.

She had been praying too long for God to do otherwise. And He had totally answered her prayers concerning her relationship with Dylan. From the beginning she asked God to guide her, protect her, and keep her heart focused on her friendship with Dylan above any other aspect of their relationship. What she had done today in letting Dylan go had been a result of that friendship. She had learned to care about him, not manipulate and control him.

She didn't want to be that kind of girl. She mentored girls like that. She wanted to give something to a relationship as well as take from it.

She wanted to give a guy what he needed from her—encouragement, friendship, sexual restraint, and the expectation he would give her the same.

But her feelings of peace didn't keep her from going to Lauren's cabin when they returned to camp so she could cry on her shoulder. Lauren had told her to stop by, and it was only ten-thirty, so she knew Lauren wouldn't be asleep yet.

She was surprised when Lauren didn't come to the door. She opened it and went inside but found the cabin dark and empty. Supposing Lauren must be at the staff lounge, unless she had gone with a group to see a movie or something, she went to her cabin, checked back fifteen minutes later, and then decided to go look for her.

Lauren wasn't at the staff lounge either, but Jessica and Chad were, and she smiled and went to join them. They seemed to be having an enjoyable evening together.

"Hey," Jessica said when she saw her, rising from Chad's side to give her a hug. "How did it go?"

"We broke up," she said simply.

"Oh, no. Really? Are you okay?"

"I'm fine," she said. "Dylan met someone in Guatemala."

"He did? And you're okay with that?"

"Sure. That's what we decided—to remain together unless one of us met someone else this summer. I think we were both a little surprised it turned out to be Dylan," she laughed. "But I'm really happy for him. We had a good day."

"That's what I was praying for," she said, sitting beside Chad once again. "For you to have a good day no matter what."

Kerri smiled. "And what did the two of you do today?"

Jessica smiled at Chad. "We went to the reservoir and came back here to do our laundry and hang out for awhile, and then we went into town for dinner."

"Just the two of you?"

"Yes."

Kerri looked at Chad and laughed. He gave her a little smile. "Did you hear someone told on you?"

"Yes, I heard," he said.

"But you didn't mind getting asked out?"

"Actually, he asked me first," Jessica interrupted. "I told him I wanted to talk to him before the meeting this morning, and he said he had something he wanted to ask me first."

"How long have you been back from town?" she asked.

Chad checked the time. "About two hours," he said.

"Have either of you seen Lauren?"

"No," Jessica replied.

"I saw her," Chad said. "But it was before dinner. She was doing her laundry."

"Do you know if a group went to see a movie or something?"

"Not that I know of," Chad said. "When we left for dinner it was deserted around here. But Adam's truck was gone. Maybe she went somewhere with him."

"Adam? Why would she go with him?"

73

"I don't know, but when I saw her in the laundry room, he was there too. And then when she left, he followed her. I didn't see either of them after that."

***

"You want to get out of here?" Adam asked. He had been sitting with Lauren in the corner booth for so long, he wasn't sure what time it was.

"Sure," she said.

They left the restaurant, and he drove them to the park by the river a few blocks away. The clock on his dash said it was after nine. He got out of the truck and met her on the other side, taking her hand and walking along the path that led to the water. The park was large with two playgrounds, a baseball field, and the river area with picnic sites and swimming spots and wooded trails. During the summertime it was usually crowded all day, but at this time of the evening it was quiet and peaceful.

Neither of them spoke until they reached the water and found a quiet place to sit on the grassy bank. She sat a little bit away from him, and he made a point of moving closer. She was affecting him physically and emotionally, and he liked the feelings her nearness stirred within him.

"Tell me about your family," he said. "Is it just you and Blake?"

"Yes," she said. "Now anyway. We had a younger brother, but he died when I was thirteen."

"How?"

"It was a freak accident. We were at the beach, and me and him were playing on a log that had washed ashore, only it wasn't completely out of the water so it would move whenever a wave came in. A really big wave hit, and we both fell off and it rolled on top of him. He was only ten and it killed him instantly."

"Wow, that must have been rough."

"Yeah, it was. I can talk about it now, but for a long time I couldn't. Not only was I right there to see him get crushed, but I felt like it was my fault because I was supposed to be watching him while my parents were in town."

"Where was Blake?"

"He wasn't there. It was during the summer, and he was working, so he didn't come with us. We were just there for the weekend."

"How did you get over it, or are you?"

"I came to the point where I truly believed Kurt was in Heaven and that God had a reason for taking him. For a long time the only image I had in my head was of him lying there lifeless on the beach, but then I went through counseling with my pastor, and he told me to pray and ask God for some images of where Kurt is now, and a few nights later I had this dream where I was talking to Kurt in Heaven, and he was telling me all about it. That might sound crazy, but I believe it was real and God gave me a glimpse of Heaven in my dreams. I've been really at peace with it ever since."

There was something about the way Lauren said things that made him want to know more. With a lot of girls he found himself tolerating their endless chatter and not hearing most of what they said, but with Lauren she always left him hanging on her next words, and he often had to prompt her to speak them.

"Do you tell everyone that or only certain people?"

She lifted her eyes to look at him. "Besides my family and my pastor, I've never told anyone that."

"Why me?"

"I don't know. I like talking to you, and you asked."

"Can I ask you something else?"

"Sure."

"What are you doing with the rest of your life?"

She laughed. "I don't know."

"Do you want to get married?"

"To you?" she asked.

He smiled. "No, just in general."

"Yeah, I think so."

"Do you want to have kids?"

"Yes."

"Do you have big career dreams?"

"No, not really. I've tried to make myself be interested in different things, but right now I feel pretty clueless about what I want."

"Besides marriage and children? There's nothing wrong with that, Lauren. That's what my mom chose. She says it's the toughest and most rewarding job there is."

"I know. My mom did too, but try telling a career counselor that. I can't wait to get to college and have yet another one tell me, 'That's nice, but you should have something to fall back on in case Prince Charming never comes along, or you think he does but leaves you penniless with three kids to take care of by yourself.'"

Adam had been attracted to many girls, but he had never experienced what he felt with Lauren. He wanted to take care of her. He wanted to be a man who would be worthy of her time and love. He didn't know if he was meant to marry her, but he knew he wanted the very best for her. Someone who would be there thirty years from now and bring a lot of joy and happiness to her life.

They were both quiet again for a few moments, but his silence wasn't a result of Lauren's words—well, it was, but not for the reason Lauren was thinking.

"I'm sorry, Adam. That's probably more than you wanted to know about me on the first date."

She was sitting with her knees tucked into her chest. He was close beside her with his legs stretched out in front of him and his hands behind him for support. Moving his left hand from the ground to her back, he stroked it gently all the way up to her hairline and back down. Sitting forward, he slipped his other hand in front of her waist and pulled her gently against him.

"I like your honesty, Lauren. I like that you don't pretend to be someone you're not."

She looked at him. He liked having her so close.

"Do you like me holding you like this?"

"Yes."

"May I kiss you right now?"

She smiled. "I don't know. I just noticed you today, and I haven't decided if I like you yet."

"I like you," he said. "Is that close enough?"

"Okay. Maybe a kiss will convince me."

He kissed her gently, and he was amazed at how easy and right it felt, as if he had done so hundreds of times before. She had an innocence that told him she hadn't done this very often, but she was certainly good at it.

"What do you think?" he said softly. "Are you ever going to let me do that again?"

"Oh, I think so," she said, giving him a gentle smile.

"Right now?"

Her smile didn't fade. "If you want to."

He kissed her again, and he didn't stop for a long time. He couldn't. She had stolen his heart today, and he didn't want it back. He wanted her to have it forever.

Chapter Nine

"It's almost eleven, Matt," Mandy said. "You should go."

They were sitting on the tailgate of a staff-member's truck in the parking lot of the camp. He gave her several more kisses and then reluctantly agreed. "I know. But I don't want to."

"Seth will get worried if you're late, and you'll have to explain this."

"We're just kissing," he said.

"Yeah, for like an hour," she laughed, not wanting him to go either but knowing he had to. She didn't want him rushing to get back to camp on time. "Please go," she said, slipping out of his arms and jumping to the ground. "For me? I don't want to have to worry about you."

"Okay," he said, scooting off the tailgate and closing it. He gave her one last kiss and held her close. "I'll try to call you sometime. I'm going to miss you very much."

"The next time we see each other, we won't have to say good-bye again. Keep thinking about that."

He walked her to the girls' cabin area and said good-night to her there. She backed away from him and blew him a kiss before turning around and jogging to her cabin so he would get out of here. She prayed, asking God to keep him from driving too fast and to keep him safe. She was getting to the point where she believed Matthew wasn't going to suddenly dump her one day, but she had this little fear he would be taken from her in some other way. She couldn't help it. He seemed too good to be true.

She hadn't been worried about today—about having a whole day with him without others around to keep them from getting carried away physically, but now that the day had ended and Matt had been so great, she whispered a prayer of thanks. She believed in waiting until marriage for anything beyond kissing, but she also felt weak with Matt. He was a good kisser, and she could imagine anything more being pleasurable as well. She prayed about it a lot. If he remained strong, she would be fine. She would never ask him to do something he shouldn't. But if he began to push things, she didn't know if she would want to stop him.

Going to the shower-house to wash her face and brush her teeth, she was happy to see Jennifer there. Jenn had become her best friend at camp this summer, and Jenn wanted to hear about her day with Matt. She told her most of what they had done and private details of what he said about falling in love and their future together. She wasn't certain if she wanted to marry Matthew Abramson yet, but she hoped she would have the chance to give it serious consideration.

After saying good-night to Jenn, she went to her cabin, got into her pajamas, and laid on her bed to write Matt a letter. She wrote him every day even though he only wrote her about twice a week. She knew he wasn't a great letter-writer. He expressed himself better face-to-face, but she loved writing to him, and he said he loved reading them, so she hadn't stopped.

Dear Matthew,

Thanks for a great day. It was even better than I imagined it would be. You are a gentleman, and I felt safe with you all day long. Thanks for that. I love your kisses, and I'm glad I can enjoy them without having to worry you're going to try anything else. And I appreciate you telling me you want me to go to Seth and ask him to talk to you if that ever changes. Not that I think I'll ever have to, but it's nice to know you would understand if I did.

One of the things I kept thinking today I never said—remember, you're the conversationalist, and I'm the writer—is it doesn't bother me that you're broke. I am too, and I don't care if you have money to spend on me. I would rather have you working a volunteer job at camp and be doing what God wants you to do than be working somewhere else just so you could take me places besides the beach and the park. And the same will be true once we get to school. If you need to work to help pay for school, I understand, but don't work a bunch of extra hours for me. I'd rather have time with you than gifts and special dates.

I also want to share something with you I'd like you to pray about. I'm starting to get scared about college. Not about being there and living away from home——I used to worry about what that would be like because I'm not great around new people, but I think God has definitely surrounded me with plenty of good friends! But what I am worried about is not knowing what I want to do with my life. I feel like I've been given this huge opportunity to go to a great school and not have to pay a dime, but I'm afraid of wasting it by choosing the wrong major or burning out on school and hating it.

I'm thinking I'd like to do more with my piano skills, but what? Becoming a concert pianist sounds like a lot of hard work and boring. Speaking of boring, you're probably getting bored with this letter. Sorry it's not more romantic, but I just needed to vent a little. Thanks for listening.

Until tomorrow,
Mandy

***

Kerri finally heard a knock on her door at eleven forty-five. Hurrying to the door and opening it, she saw Lauren standing there, and she gave her an immediate hug.

"Where have you been? I was getting worried."

Lauren laughed. "Sorry. I would have left a note, but I had no idea we would be getting back this late."

"We?"

Lauren sighed and put her hands over her face. Peeking through her fingers and dropping her hands, she said what Kerri expected her to say.

"I spent the day with Adam."

"The day!" she laughed, pulling her inside. "How did that happen?"

"Why don't you sound surprised?"

"Chad said he saw you together this afternoon, and then when you weren't here and Adam wasn't either, I assumed you were with him."

"It was crazy," she said, shaking her head and smiling. "I feel like I'm dreaming."

"Lauren!" she laughed. "I'm gone for one day and you end up with Adam?"

Lauren told her the whole story, from meeting Adam in the staff lounge before lunch, to shopping together, to returning to do their laundry, and then him asking her out for dinner.

"And what have you been doing since dinner?" Kerri asked, loving the sound of this story and Lauren's excitement about it. She knew Lauren hadn't dated much, and she hadn't gone out with any guys this summer or expressed an interest in anyone.

"We talked for a long time after having pizza," she said. "And then we went to the park—the one in town by the river—and," she said shyly, "we sat by the river and he kissed me."

"More than once?"

"Yes," she said.

"For how long?"

"About an hour," she said.

Kerri laughed. "An hour? Please tell me Adam behaved himself."

"He did, Kerri. I promise. I never would have stayed that long with him otherwise. We didn't just kiss. We talked and he held me. It was nice. Really. I'm just in shock he feels that way about me."

"Why wouldn't he? You're sweet and fun, and Adam is the same way. I think you're perfect for each other. I'm shocked Adam was so bold. He's a bit on the shy side around girls."

"He wasn't today. I think because it started as going into town to get lunch together. We were the only ones still here, and then it was like neither of us wanted it to end."

"I'm happy if you're happy," she said, giving her a hug. "And if he starts being a jerk, I know him well enough to give him a piece of my mind. You can tell him I said that."

"Okay, I will," she said. "What about you? How was your day?"

"Not as good as yours."

Lauren lost her smile. "What happened?"

"At first I thought things were fine," she said, going on to tell her everything.

"How do you feel now?"

"It's strange. I felt happy we were together when it seemed like things were going to continue between us, but then when he told me the truth, I felt okay with that too. Honestly, he's a great guy and I'd be blessed to have him, but the bottom-line is I want him to be with the right girl. And I don't think this is going to hit me harder tomorrow or next week. I feel like God prepared me for it. I had prayed that whatever was supposed to happen today would happen and I'd have peace about it, and that's what He gave me."

"If you need to talk, I'm here," Lauren said. "But otherwise I won't bug you about it. You are the most emotionally stable friend I've ever had."

After Lauren headed for bed, Kerri thought about what Lauren had said, and she hadn't thought about it before, but she did tend to remain steady in her emotional health no matter what was going on around her. She had been frazzled this morning, but that was rare for her. In reality, being with Dylan and often not knowing what to do had caused her more stress than anything she had ever encountered, and in a way it was a relief to let him go.

But she knew she would miss him, and once again she was back to waiting for the right guy to walk into her life. Had she already met him and not seen him that way? Would she be meeting him in another month at Lifegate? Or would she be waiting for years?

When she turned out the light and snuggled under her warm comforter, she prayed silently for a few minutes, asking God to give her peace and fill the void Dylan's absence would leave. And then she allowed herself to cry.

For the last two years she had been watching her brother and Amber fall in love and have a completely wonderful relationship. She wanted that for herself. She wanted it at the right time and with the right person, but still, she wanted it, and she wasn't afraid to let God know. Through her words. Through her tears. And by taking the hope He gave her and tucking it deep inside her heart.

Chapter Ten

Lauren walked to her cabin after saying good-night to Kerri, grabbed her bath caddy, and headed for the restroom down the hill. While brushing her teeth in the deserted common bathroom, she tried to keep the thought that had entered her mind five minutes ago from making it to her lips, but after spitting out the toothpaste, rinsing her mouth, and looking at herself in the mirror, she whispered the words.

"I'm going to lose him."

The thought brought a deep pain to her heart. She had never had a day like today. She'd been completely swept off her feet by Adam. It had been a dream come true, only she had never imagined having such a perfect and passionate first date with him.

But that was when he thought he could never have Kerri. He had settled for someone who was waiting in the wings because she was here and Kerri wasn't and Kerri was already taken. But now she wasn't. There was no boyfriend back home to keep Adam from asking her out.

She went to bed and couldn't sleep. She usually went to bed early and slept easily, but her emotions were on a roller coaster. One minute she was remembering Adam's sweet kisses and tender touch and affectionate words, and the next she was preparing herself for the reality she would never have times like that again. Even if Adam pretended to want to be with her instead of Kerri, he wouldn't be able to fake the kind of kisses he had given her today. She would know it, and letting him go would be her only option.

Even if Kerri rejected him, she wouldn't want him back. She didn't want to be anyone's second choice. And in reality she already was. How had she let Adam kiss her so freely? How had she allowed herself to believe he really wanted her?

"You're making me feel things I've never felt before, Lauren," he'd said. "I can't get enough of your sweet lips. I've never kissed a girl like this before, and it's better than I ever imagined it would be."

All summer she had been watching Adam and waiting for him to notice her, and he finally had. But tomorrow her heartbreak would be excruciating when she saw the look in his eyes. Once he learned about what had happened today between Kerri and Dylan, he wouldn't be able to hide his true wishes from her. She had been watching those eyes, waiting for them to look at her the way he looked at Kerri. He'd done so today, but that would end tomorrow. She felt sure of it.

***

On Sunday morning Mandy slept in. Chapel wasn't until ten o'clock, and she didn't feel hungry enough to get out of bed to have breakfast served at eight. She dozed back off but was interrupted before her alarm awakened her at the new time.

"Mandy, wake up, honey," someone said, shaking her shoulder.

She opened her eyes and saw her senior counselor. Thinking she must have overslept, she sat up quickly and apologized, but Alicia seemed to be looking at her a little too seriously for sleeping late.

"There's a phone call for you," she said. "Up at the office. The person said it's urgent."

Throwing on her jeans and putting her coat over her pajama top, she hurried out of the cabin and up the hill, her mind swimming with the frightening possibilities. Had something happened to one of her family members? Her mom and dad, sister, or brother? An accident? Matt? Had he driven too fast? Her cousin Amber and Seth? They'd gone to Portland yesterday and were planning to drive home late too.

Picking up the phone in the vacant office, she said hello to the caller with a trembling voice. It was Amber, and she had a sinking feeling. If anyone would be calling her about Matt, it would be her.

"What happened?" she asked. "Is it Matt?"

"Yes," Amber said. "I thought I should call you. I'm guessing no one else has?"

"No. Is he hurt or—" She couldn't finish her thought.

"No, it's not him," Amber said. "I'm sorry, I'm not good with stuff like this. It's his brother. Mark. He was killed last night."

Mandy gasped. "What? How?"

"He got hit by a car. They're not exactly sure what happened. His dad called Dave in the middle of the night. Matt wanted to go right away, so Seth went with him."

Matthew's brother, Mark, was fifteen and he'd been in and out of trouble lately. Matt had been worried about him, and she didn't know if him getting hit by a car had anything to do with his reckless behavior, but either way she couldn't imagine what Matt must be feeling right now. She felt like this had to be a nightmare. Was she dreaming? Had all of her fears about losing Matt led to this? Slowly letting the news sink in and facing the reality Mark was really dead, she knew she had to go be with Matt, but she didn't have a way to get there by herself. She could probably borrow someone's car, but she didn't want to go alone.

"If you want to, I could drive Seth's car and go up with you," Amber offered.

"Yes, I want to," she said.

"I'll be there in an hour, okay, sweetie?"

"Okay," she said.

Hanging up the phone, Mandy didn't know what to do except pray. She prayed for Matt and his family. Matt and his younger brother were the only children. When her grandpa had died last year, that had been a difficult time for her, but she hadn't been as close to Grandpa Smith as Matt was to Mark, and her grandfather had lived a good, long life, not been killed at fifteen.

Leaving the office, she went to find Isaac, the camp director she had been working under for the past three years, and told him the news. He understood her desire to go, telling her to let them know if and when she would return. He said they would be praying for her, as well as Matt and his family, and he did so with her right then, giving her peace as she went to her cabin and got her things together.

Someone would be taking over her cabin this week until she could return—if she did. She was willing to forgo her last week of camp and remain with Matt instead, but she didn't know if he would want her to. She felt nervous about seeing him. Sometimes Matt could close himself off from others if he didn't want to talk about something, but she wanted to be there for him.

Jenn and Jeremiah came by her cabin while she was packing. They'd heard the news, and they came to offer their support and told her they would be praying. They had both become really good friends to her this summer, and she realized she might not see them again if she didn't return before the weekend. She gave them hugs good-bye now in case that happened.

She didn't have to wait long for Amber to arrive, and when Amber got out of the car to meet her, she lost it. The reality of what had happened hit her fully, and she felt an incredible amount of pain for Matt. Amber held her close.

"What am I going to say, Amber? I don't know if I can do this."

"Just be there, Mandy. When Grandpa died, that was all I needed from Seth."

Once they were on the road, neither of them said anything until Amber broke the silence. "Would you like to hear some good news?"

"Sure," she said.

"Colleen and Blake went to Crater Lake together yesterday and had a really nice time."

"What's that mean—she finally let him kiss her?"

"Yes!"

"What about Chris? Does she miss him at all?"

"I think she does. But she sees their lives heading in different directions, and even though she wasn't looking for anything to happen with Blake, it is anyway. She told me with Chris it was more about having a relationship, but Blake is touching her heart on a deeper level—in a way she can't describe."

Mandy thought about her own relationship with Matt. Since he was her first boyfriend, she didn't have anything to compare their relationship to, but Matt did, and he'd said something similar to her yesterday. Whenever they were together, he entered a completely different world: a place he loved to be, and she knew she felt the same way.

Maybe he would push her away today and not let her into his painful world, or maybe she could take him to another one. *Help me to be whatever Matthew needs me to be today, Jesus. May I be a source of peace and comfort, or just stay out of the way if that's what I need to do. I have no idea what to say. Why did this have to happen? Who am I to be his girlfriend at a time like this? Please help me.*

***

The mood of the morning at Camp Laughing Water became subdued as word got around about Matt's brother. Blake was busy trying to figure out whom he was going to put in to replace two of his key counselors for the week. Seth had said he might be back by this afternoon, but Blake didn't expect him to be. He could understand if Seth chose to spend the week with his best friend who had lost his brother. He knew what that kind of pain was like, and whether Matt admitted it or not, he would need the support of his close friends.

When Blake saw Lauren heading for the staff lounge with Kerri for breakfast, he knew she had heard the news from Kerri, who had been informed of the tragedy early this morning along with Amber. He also knew this could hit Lauren harder than most because of their similar experience five years ago with Kurt.

His sister saw him coming, and she hurried toward him, giving him a hug and allowing him to hold her for a long time.

"When did you hear?" he asked.

"About an hour ago."

"You okay?"

She shrugged. "Sure does bring back memories in a hurry, huh?"

"Yep."

"Did you talk to Matt before they left?"

"Yes. Dave got me up first and then Seth, and we all told him together."

"I'm sorry, Blake," she said. "Just hearing about it was more than enough for me."

Blake heard someone coming up the path, and he saw Adam for only a brief second before Adam gently grasped Lauren's arm and spoke to her.

"Hey," he said, giving her a hug. "Are you okay?"

Blake wondered why Adam would be so concerned about his sister, and how he would know why this news might affect her more than the average staff member, but he let Lauren speak for herself.

"Not really," she said, breaking into quiet tears.

Adam let her cry on his shoulder and seemed very concerned for her, shutting his eyes and gently rocking her from side to side. Blake wasn't aware of his sister having such a close relationship with Adam and wondered how long that had been going on. Not that he objected. Not at all. Adam was one of his best counselors and an all-around decent guy.

Without saying anything, he stepped away and gave them privacy, wondering if Kerri had any insight to share on this new development. Lauren hadn't told him anything about Adam, but maybe she had told her best friend.

Chapter Eleven

"I just heard," Adam said. "When did you?"

Lauren looked into Adam's eyes and answered, feeling unsure about why she had fallen apart like that. She had cried earlier with Kerri and thought she'd gotten it all out, but apparently not.

"After I got up this morning," she said. "Kerri told me."

"I feel awful for Matt, but I immediately thought of you. Do a lot of people here know about Kurt?"

"Not really," she said. "It's not something I tell everybody, although I'm not sure who Blake has told in the past. More might know than I think."

"Is there anything I can do, Lauren? Anything you need from me?"

"I think you just gave it to me," she said, stepping forward and hugging him this time. He held her gently in return. "I'll be all right. I'm just hurting for Matt. I know what he's feeling."

Adam didn't say anything else on the subject, but after a few moments of silence, he said something that made her heart feel lighter. Under normal circumstances, holding each other for an extended amount of time would be against camp rules, but

Adam was taking advantage of the excuse to extend his stay.

"I thought about you all night. And I missed you already by this morning."

She smiled, realizing her brother had stepped away. "I think you're going to have some explaining to do to your senior counselor."

"You didn't tell him?"

"I didn't have a chance."

Adam stepped back and smiled. "I won't mind telling him."

A mixture of joy and pain filled Lauren's heart. Adam was being as sweet and caring as he'd been last night, but he didn't know about Kerri yet. She had planned to tell him sometime this morning, but she couldn't go there with her emotions already thrown for a loop today. She decided to wait and let him find out some other way and then deal with however that news affected him.

"Are you hungry?" he asked.

She nodded and they stepped toward the staff lounge. Going inside, they both took some food from the counter and looked around for a place to sit. The atmosphere was unusually quiet, and since the couch area where Blake, Kerri, and others were sitting was full, Adam led her over to one of the unoccupied window-seats.

Lauren knew others' eyes were on them. She caught Kerri's smile from across the room, and her friend winked at her. Lauren glanced at Adam to see if he had seen it, but his eyes were on her. She knew she should tell him and get it over with, but Adam said something to divert her thoughts.

"Are you regretting what happened between us last night, Angel? I hope you're not, but if you are, I want you to tell me."

"I'm not," she said. "Are you?"

"No. Definitely not."

She decided to say it. "Even if you knew Kerri broke up with her boyfriend yesterday?"

He smiled. "Did she?" Adam glanced at Kerri and then back to her. "Don't you love the way God works?"

"What's that mean?"

"He helped me to see you at just the right time. If we hadn't spent the day together, I'd be wasting my energy obsessing over her for another six months. But she's not for me, Angel. You are."

"Are you sure about that?"

He smiled. "Yes."

"How do you know?"

He whispered his answer in her ear. "Because your lips are my favorite flavor."

She laughed. Last night he kept telling her they were different flavors, and when she finally said, 'Okay, what's your verdict? Which flavor are they?' he'd said, 'My favorite.'

Blake came over to sit with them, taking a folding chair from the wall and interrupting their private conversation.

"Okay, so the rumor is my sister spent the better part of yesterday with you, Buzz Lightyear. Is this true?"

"Yes."

"And what do you have to say for yourself?"

"Good move, Adam?"

Blake smiled. "And what about you, little sister? What do you have to say for yourself? I thought you were going to stay here and rest."

"Ummm, I was kidnapped by a space ranger?"

Blake rolled his eyes, and Lauren saw Colleen step through the door. She knew they had gone to Crater Lake yesterday, and she wondered how that had turned out.

"What did Pocahontas think of our backyard wonder?"

Blake's eyes lit up. "I think she liked it."

"Have you heard from Seth?" Adam asked, turning the topic back to the solemn news of the morning.

"I talked to him an hour ago," Blake said. "They made it there, and Matt is with his family. Amber went to pick up Matt's girlfriend, and they're on their way now. Seth and Amber might be back today, depending on how things go, but I told them to stay if they feel like they should."

When Adam and Lauren had finished eating their fruit and donuts, they headed for the meeting room where they normally gathered for Sunday morning worship, but the format was different than usual. Justin had put together the worship stations like he sometimes did for the campers during the week, giving them each freedom to worship and pray as they felt individually led to do so. Lauren spent a lot of time at the prayer benches, asking God to comfort Matt and his family and to help those who were surrounding them to know how to help.

Dave had them all form a circle at the end of the hour and hold hands as he said a group prayer for Matt, his family, and Mark's friends who had witnessed the accident. The details of what had happened still weren't clear, but Lauren could imagine more than one person pointing the finger at themselves as the one to blame. She prayed for whomever they were.

***

Amber drove to Seth's house and went inside to see if he was here or if he was at Matt's. If he wasn't, she needed to get directions anyway because she had never driven there on her own. Mandy waited in the car for Amber to return, and she did less than a minute later.

"Seth's here," she said. "He came home to have something to eat and wait for us. Are you hungry? We could eat before we go over to Matt's."

"I didn't have breakfast," she said, getting out of the car and following Amber inside. "Does Matt know I'm coming?"

"Yes. Seth told him. He was sleeping when he left, and Matt's mom said she would call when he woke up."

They ate sandwiches that Mrs. Kirkwood made for them, and Seth told them what he knew about the accident. According to Mark's friends, they had gone to a party last night Mark's parents weren't aware he was at. They thought he had gone to the movies. Mark and his friends had been drinking, and one of Mark's friends ran the car off the road into a ditch on the way home. No one had been hurt, and they all got out to walk the rest of the way. Mark had wandered into the street, just playing around, and a car had come around a corner and hit him.

"How's Matt?" Mandy asked.

"Not good," Seth said in a way Mandy knew he was not good at all. "He mostly wanted to be alone once we got there. I talked to him some, but he's not ready to hear anything right now."

"Do you think he wants me here? Honestly? If you think it's better if I wait until tomorrow or longer, I will."

Seth reached over and laid his hand on hers. "Honestly Mandy, I don't know. But I think you should try to see him today. He knows you're coming."

"Did he ask you to call me?"

Seth avoided the question. "I think it's worth a shot. He needs to let someone in."

Mandy agreed to go. She had to try, and they left after they finished eating. His mom hadn't called, but Seth thought she might be sleeping now too. They had been up most of the night.

When the three of them arrived at the house, Seth went inside without waiting for anyone to let him in. He returned a few minutes later and said he'd found Matt awake and sitting on the floor in Mark's bedroom. He hadn't talked to him, but he thought she should go in—alone.

Mandy didn't know if she liked that option. But Seth knew Matt better than anyone, so she agreed to go inside and talk to him. Getting out of the car, she prayed with every step she took.

She had only been to Matt's house a couple of times, but she knew all three bedrooms were upstairs: Matt's, his parents', and Mark's. She could hear voices coming from the kitchen and family room area at the back of the house, but she went up the stairs and walked to the end of the hall. Matt's bedroom was on the left overlooking the street, and Mark's was on the right. She paused for a moment when she reached it and said a silent prayer.

I don't know what to say, Jesus. Please help. Fill me with your Spirit right now and let your words flow through me.

The door to Mark's bedroom was partially open, and she pushed it further, far enough to see Matt sitting on the floor, leaning against the footboard of Mark's bed with his forehead resting on his bent knees and his hands on the side of his head.

She slipped inside and closed the door behind her. Matt didn't look up, and she went to him, kneeling on the floor when she got to his side. He didn't move, and she spoke softly.

"Hey, it's me," she said, stroking the back of his dark hair. "I'm here, Matthew. I'm so sorry. I came as soon as I heard."

He didn't respond. She had no idea what to say. The closeness they'd had yesterday was swallowed up in grief, and she didn't know how to get it back or if she should try. Maybe yesterday and their entire relationship was a fairy-tale with no ties to the harsh reality of life.

"Please look at me, Matthew," she whispered. "If you want to tell me to go away, then do that, but don't pretend I'm not here."

He lifted his head and leaned it against the bed. He opened his eyes, but he didn't look at her. "I told them not to call you."

She wasn't completely surprised by his words because of what Seth had said, but hearing him say he didn't want her to be here was shocking because of how close they had become. He wasn't himself, and she wasn't sure how to speak to this Matthew, but she tried anyway.

She placed her hand on his cheek and turned his face toward her. His eyes were dark and lifeless. "Why didn't you want them to call me?"

"Because you shouldn't be here, Amanda," he said evenly but not harshly. "You shouldn't be anywhere near me."

She had seen this self-condemning side of him once before. He had a fight with his parents before coming out to see her one Saturday, and after cooling off from that he admitted he had been wrong and had lied to them like they'd accused him of. He said to her, 'I don't think I'm the guy you want to be with, Amanda. You deserve someone better than me. I'm not the person I was six months ago, but I'm not all I should be either.'

She had told him she was willing to take her chances. She was a work-in-progress too, and nobody was perfect. She knew a different response was needed now, but her triumph in that moment gave her courage to try this time too.

"I had to come, Matt. I want to be here."

"You shouldn't."

"Why not?"

"Just go, Amanda," he said, lowering her hand from his face and releasing her fingers. "I need to do this on my own."

She didn't say anything, but his words of dismissal weren't convincing. She knew he didn't really want her to go. Turning her body slightly, she leaned against the bed and sat as close to him as possible.

"Well, that's too bad, Matthew, because I won't let you. You can put on a tough-guy act with everyone else, but not with me."

"Amanda," he sighed. "I want you to go."

"I don't believe you," she said, lifting his arm and putting it around her shoulders so she could lean into him fully.

He didn't resist her, and she wasn't going to leave unless he literally kicked her out of the room. She laid her head on his chest, and he gave in, holding on to her desperately. He started crying. She let him without saying anything.

When his body relaxed some, she tilted her face toward him and kissed his lips before he could stop her. She had to work a little bit to get him to kiss her back, but he did eventually. He stopped after a few moments, buried his face in her neck, and cried more. It wasn't the first time she had heard Matt cry. He had a couple of times when he'd confessed the mistakes of his past, but these were different— mournful and unstoppable.

"It's my fault, Amanda," he said. "I killed my little brother."

"It's not your fault, Matthew," she said, stroking his cheek that needed a shave.

"It is. I wasn't a good example for him. I—"

"Shh," she said, trying to kiss him again.

He pushed her away this time and scrambled to his feet. "It is, Amanda! Mark is dead, and it's my fault."

His abruptness didn't faze her. This was an unpeaceful situation, and Matt was acting in a way she had never seen before, but she had peace. She didn't know why, but she did. She gave him a moment but then rose to her feet and stepped over to where he had stopped in front of the window. She placed herself in the space between him and the glass and gently took his hands.

"Matthew. Look at me."

He lowered his eyes from where they were gazing out the window. His jaw twitched, and he looked angry, but she knew he wasn't mad at her. He was mad at himself and possibly Mark. He had tried to talk to him about the choices he was making, but Mark simply hadn't listened.

"Where is Mark right now?"

Matt didn't respond.

"Where is he, Matthew?"

He remained silent, but she knew he was thinking it.

"In Heaven?"

Matt took a deep breath and sighed. "Yes."

"And who is he with?"

"God," Matt whispered.

"And is that a good place for him to be? Is he safe there? Is he happy?"

Matt allowed tears to fall from his eyes and run down his cheeks.

"He's not there because of you, Matthew. He's there because God took him. And we will miss him, and yes, he died in a tragic and senseless way, but that's our perspective, not God's."

He seemed to be listening, and she continued with her thoughts.

"God has him, Matt. He didn't let go. Mark's there with Jesus right now. And he's safe, and he's all right. Isn't that what we believe? Isn't that what Jesus died for, to set us free from death being the final destination? Isn't that what we've been working at camp all summer to teach kids—that there's hope? That death is not the end? That we can have eternity with God even if we mess up our life here on earth?"

Matt swallowed hard and the tears continued to fall. He wrapped his arms around her and pulled her close to him. She could feel the anger and guilt and heaviness flowing out of his rigid body, and within seconds the familiar gentleness of Matt's arms were surrounding her.

"It's okay, Matthew," she said and waited for him to release her. When he did, he replaced his embrace with kisses and gentle words.

"I love you, Amanda. I love you, and I need you."

She kissed him in return, and she felt a oneness—a closeness she hadn't felt with him before.

"Do you have to go back today?" he asked.

"I can stay as long as you want me to."

"That's going to be all week."

"I'm here, Matthew," she whispered. "I love you too, and I'm not going anywhere."

Chapter Twelve

Amber and Seth stayed at Matt's house for the afternoon before deciding to head back to camp. Having three counselors gone during high school camp would put a strain on the staff, and Matt didn't want them sitting around holding his hand.

"Mandy's here," he told them. "I'll be all right."

Mandy had a unique feeling as she listened to Matt saying he wanted her here more than his best friend who had been through so much with him. She knew she reached a part of his heart others couldn't, even Seth. She didn't understand why, but she wasn't going to argue with him. She wanted to be as much of a part of his life as he would allow her to be. And while she never would have chosen for this to happen to his brother, she could already see this was going to bring them closer.

The next twenty-four hours proved it. She didn't do much except be with him and listen when he felt like talking, but since he didn't crawl back into his shell and push everyone away, she supposed that was enough. They mostly hung around the house. Matt liked to go into Mark's bedroom and talk about all the good times they'd had growing up rather than his more recent difficulties. He had moments when a fresh wave a grief would hit him, and he would let the tears come. She remained by his side and held him but didn't say a lot.

On Monday night she was sleeping in Matt's room, and Matt was sleeping in Mark's like he'd done the night before. He said being in there made him feel closer to Mark and brought him comfort, so she hadn't insisted on sleeping on the couch so he could have his own bed. She heard him crying in the hallway at two a.m. and went out to sit with him until he stopped.

"You can have your bed, and I'll go downstairs," she said. She thought it was fine for Matt to sleep in his brother's room, but she didn't think it would be appropriate for her to do so, and she wasn't sure she could go to sleep if she did.

"I'll sleep in my bed if you do too," he said.

She knew he was back to his playful self. "No way. You would hog the blankets. I know it."

He smiled and gave her a brief kiss. "I'm all right," he said. "Go back to bed, and I'll see you in the morning."

"We could go to my house tomorrow if you want to get away."

"Maybe on Wednesday," he said. "My mom wants to put that cross by the road sometime tomorrow."

"Has she been in Mark's room at all?"

"I don't think so. And she hasn't slept much. I think she's downstairs right now. I'm going to go sit with her. You go back to sleep, baby."

She did go back to bed, but she laid awake, wondering what it would be like if she lost one of her siblings. She had been away from both of them quite a bit now with being at camp, her older sister being married, and her brother away at college for the past two years. And going to college in California herself would mean she would be seeing even less of them. She missed them, but they were only a phone call or online message away, and she saw them on major holidays and other times throughout the year. Matt would never have that with Mark again.

On Tuesday morning before lunch, Matt left with his parents to go put the cross beside the road where Mark had been killed, and Mandy stayed behind. When Matt told her his mom wanted it to just be the three of them, she felt a little hurt, but she understood his grieving mother's wishes, and she used the opportunity to call her mom and dad and talk to them for longer than she had thus far.

T.J. was home this summer, working with Dad doing kitchen and bathroom remodeling—something her dad did in the summer to make extra income while he wasn't teaching. But her brother wasn't there when she called. He had gone to pick up supplies they needed for a job they were doing later in the week.

She told them she might be out tomorrow, but she wasn't sure. If she didn't go, she supposed it would be sometime this weekend or next week before she would have a chance to go home. The memorial service was scheduled for Thursday, and she wanted to be with Matt as long as he needed her. He hadn't decided if he was going back to camp for the final week or not, nor had she decided if she was going on her staff retreat this weekend. She wanted to because she wouldn't be seeing her friends there again for awhile—if ever, but she didn't want it badly enough to leave Matt if he needed her to stay.

That afternoon she learned something she hadn't known: Mark was supposed to be at Camp Laughing Water this week. He had signed up to go with the group from their church, and he would have been there on Sunday afternoon if the accident hadn't happened the night before.

"You should go to camp and talk about it," she said.

"What do you mean?" Matt asked.

"I mean sometime this week. Maybe Friday night. You could talk about the bad choices he was making and how it cost him his life, but then also share about the hope you have he's with God. I'm sure it would be very powerful—especially since he was supposed to be there. It might make someone think."

He sighed. "I'm sure you're right, but I don't think I could do it."

"Then maybe Seth could. You should talk to him about it on Thursday when he comes for the memorial service."

"He's probably already thought about it."

"He might not want to without asking you, and he might be afraid to ask—like he doesn't want you to think he's being insensitive."

They were sitting side by side at the foot of Mark's bed like they had been on Sunday afternoon and several other times. Matt turned to face her and gave her several sweet kisses. "I'm glad you're here, Amanda."

"If you want to stay here tomorrow, we can. Going to spend some time with my family was just an idea. I can see them next week."

"No, I want to go. I need to get away from here for a day."

"Am I helping, Matthew?"

"Yes, Amanda. I'm glad you're here. I just said that."

"Can I ask you something?"

"No," he said and laughed, kissing her instead of letting her speak.

It was good to hear him laugh. She smiled and waited for him to retract his answer.

"Of course you can," he said, pulling her close and holding her gently.

"What exactly is it you like about me? Why would you rather have me here than Seth? Why would you rather go with me to see my family tomorrow instead of staying here?"

"Because you make me feel whole," he said, allowing his tender emotions to surface. "I don't want to be away from you, Amanda, especially right now. But I want you to be happy, not just enduring time with me."

"I wouldn't be enduring anything if we stayed here."

"I know, but it will bring you joy to see your family, and I will soak up some for myself. Putting that cross by the road gave me a hollow and depressed feeling. I wish you would have been there. You bring peace and joy to my heart, Amanda. I knew that before this week, but now I really know it."

***

By Tuesday evening, Kerri felt emotionally drained. With the news of Matt's brother coming first thing on Sunday morning, she hadn't been able to think about her breakup with Dylan, but this afternoon she had talked to one of her high school campers coming off of a recent breakup, and she realized she was having some of the same feelings of emptiness—like a part of herself was suddenly gone. She wasn't sure if that was normal, or if she had become more attached to Dylan than she had realized.

During the evening meeting while the speaker for the week was talking, she had to get up and go outside. Her tears were mainly for Matt. He had been through so much already, had finally gotten his life straightened out, and now this had happened. Matt had asked for prayer for his brother several times this summer, and she had been praying for him. She didn't understand why God had chosen to work this way.

After a few minutes Lauren came looking for her, holding her and letting her cry. When she had calmed down some, Lauren asked if this was about Matt or Dylan or something else.

Kerri let out a cross between a laugh and a cry. "I think all three," she said. "It's just a tough day."

"What are you thinking about Dylan?"

"I don't know. I'm not sure if I miss *him*, or the idea of being in a relationship. This morning I found myself wishing I was Matt's girlfriend so I could be supporting him right now. I used to have a huge crush on him." She laughed at her admission. "I'm just a mess."

Lauren laughed. "Even you are entitled to be a mess once in awhile. You can't be perfect all the time."

"Oh, please," she said. "I am far from perfect. I think you're talking about you. And speaking of you, how are things with Adam?"

She smiled. "Good. I haven't had much time with him since Sunday morning, obviously, but we've had a few moments, and he's left several notes in my mailbox."

"Do you have any on you?"

"Yes," she said with a sweet expression.

"Well, hand it over. I'm in need of sweet words from a guy right now, even if they're not for me."

Lauren reached into her pocket and took out a folded note and held it out to her.

"I'm just kidding," she said, wanting to read it, but not wanting to invade her friend's privacy. "You shouldn't show me."

"Actually, I'll read part of it to you. He said something about Matt's brother I found comforting."

Lauren scanned the note. Finding the part she was looking for, she read it to her:

"I was thinking about Matt today and realizing we never know what tomorrow may hold. And while sometimes tragedy will come, I think far more often we are surprised with delightful moments. On Saturday I had no idea I would be kissing you by the end of the day, and I'm glad I didn't know it was coming because I think it made it more special. Even

today I didn't expect to end up in that canoe with you during the game, but suddenly there you were in the midst of the craziness, and it made my morning. I'm looking forward to many more delightful moments with you, Angel, and I wish you many sweet surprises this week. There truly is a time for everything under heaven—like that verse says, but I think God is partial to the good times, don't you? Sometimes we get so used to them, we forget all the reasons we have to smile."

Lauren refolded the letter from Adam and smiled. Kerri smiled in return and said, "I'm sorry if this week is clouding your joy with Adam. I'm really thrilled for you, and for him. I've always known he would find a very special girl someday."

"Did you ever have a crush on him?" she teased but seriously wanted to know the answer.

"Not really," she said. "He reminds me too much of Seth. It would be like dating my brother. But I have gotten to know him pretty well, and I know he's a special guy."

They went back into the meeting and waited for the speaker to finish talking before going to sit with their girls and sing a final song. Following the meeting they had a break where the campers could hang out, get something from the Snack Shack, and change into warmer clothes for campfire time.

Lauren went into the senior staff dining area off the kitchen to get hot chocolate, and Adam found her there. She didn't know if he had followed her or happened to be coming to get something too, but she was happy to see him and have a few private moments together.

"This is a nice surprise," she said, recalling the words from his letter.

He smiled. "I'm glad you think so. I'd say it's a nice surprise for me too, but I sort of followed you, so it's not really a surprise, but it's definitely a good moment."

She finished stirring her hot chocolate and decided to remain there and drink it instead of going back to her cabin like she had planned. Adam fixed himself some also and seemed perfectly happy to stand there talking to her.

"Did you put a 'Keep Out' sign on the door?" she asked. "This place is usually busier."

"No, but I thought about locking the door."

She laughed.

"Is Kerri all right? I saw you go out to check on her."

"Yeah, she's just having a tough day. I read that part of your letter to her."

"The part about how I can't wait until Saturday so I can kiss you more?" he said, tossing her a wink.

"No, the part about nice surprises."

"You liked that?"

"It was very insightful for a space ranger."

"I'm glad I've been blind to you all summer."

"Excuse me?"

"I wouldn't have been able to take this week after week. I have no idea how Seth has made it the last two summers."

"I don't know," she said. "I think this has a certain appeal—being followed into the staff kitchen and having a few stolen moments over hot chocolate."

"And stolen kisses?" he asked, stepping a little closer to her.

Secretly she knew she would love one of his kisses now, but knowing he wanted to was enough. She gave him a mild shove away from her.

"I know one thing Amber and Seth have done is meet in the mornings to read the Bible and pray together," he said seriously. "Would you like to meet me before the counselor meeting tomorrow?"

"Sure. I'd love that."

"Are you a morning person? I'm guessing you are."

"Yes," she said. "I'm ready for bed about now."

"I may be a bit bleary-eyed, but I'll be there."

"Where would you like to meet?"

"By the lake?"

"Okay."

They were interrupted then—by Blake of all people.

"Please tell me I'm not seeing this," he said, reaching for a cup and getting himself some coffee.

"Seeing what?" she said innocently. "Two staff members sharing a few moments together near the end of a busy day? Isn't that good staff relations?"

Blake laughed. "Oh, I am so not ready for this."

"Ready for what? For your sister to be dating? I'm eighteen and a half. I'd say it's about time."

"Twenty would be better," he said, giving her a kiss on the cheek. "I've got to run. If I don't see you at Fireside in twenty minutes, I'll know where to find you."

"Unless we go somewhere else," she teased him.

Adam asked her something after her brother was gone.

"You've never dated anyone before?"

"No."

"Not at all?"

She could feel her insecurities rising, but she answered him honestly. "I had one date when I was a junior. This guy asked me to meet him at a dance after the football game, and I did, but he ended up dancing with a lot of other girls more than me. Other than that? Nope. Saturday was my debut into the world of dating."

"Do you have any idea how much that shocks me?"

"Why?"

"Because you're beautiful and amazing and someone I want to kiss so badly right now I can hardly stand it."

She told him her view on why she hadn't been asked out more, feeling her fears returning that Adam may wish he had waited one more day for Kerri. "I guess I've always been the girl who guys saw as friendship material but dated or wanted to date my best friend."

She regretted her words as soon as she spoke them. What was she doing? How could she speak that way to Adam after how wonderful he had been all week?

Somehow he saw right through her accusing words to her insecure heart. Tossing his empty cup into the trash, he stepped over and gave her a gentle hug.

"I don't see you that way anymore, Angel."

She wanted to believe him, and she did, but his next words helped her a bit more.

"I'm not settling for you because I couldn't have Kerri. You don't think that, do you?"

She held in the tears, but her silence gave her away.

"I'm sorry," he whispered. "I was an idiot. It wasn't you, it was me."

She took a deep breath and stepped away. "I don't blame you for being attracted to Kerri. If I was a guy, I'm sure I would be too. I just hope—" She stopped, wondering if she really wanted to say this.

"You hope what?"

She looked into his eyes and decided to believe the guy she had been with on Saturday who had said so many sweet things was the same guy standing here right now.

"I hope you really do like me, because I really, really, really like you."

Chapter Thirteen

Adam felt amazed. He had been working at this camp for three summers, met a lot of girls he'd been attracted to on some level, but hadn't managed to find the right one for him—until now. He hadn't dated much either. A few girls back home he went out with once or twice; his first summer on staff when he dated two girls over the course of the summer who were good friends—that had been a mistake; and one girl last summer he'd been on a couple of group dates with, but it hadn't gone beyond that.

And then this year he spent almost every Saturday with Kerri and Lauren, along with whatever group they were a part of. But he had been so focused on Kerri, he completely overlooked Lauren, while she had been watching him a fair amount no less, and yet here she was, still wanting to be with him instead of calling him an idiot like he deserved.

Before he had a chance to respond to Lauren's words, they were interrupted by Seth, and then Amber less than ten seconds later, and Adam knew it wasn't likely a coincidence.

"So this is where you two find time together at the end of the day?" he said.

"Whatever works," Seth said, taking Amber into his arms and giving her a long hug. "Especially this week."

"Especially on our anniversary," Amber added.

"What anniversary?" Lauren asked.

"Of the day we first met. Two years ago today."

After exchanging their recharge hug, Amber and Seth stepped away from each other and Seth made them both hot chocolate.

"I see the rumors are true, Adam?" Amber said, smiling at him. "I heard something about you finally getting yourself a date this summer?"

"Yes, I did," he said, smiling at Lauren. "And I didn't even realize it until I was already on it."

Amber laughed and Lauren did too.

"And," he added. "I've never been so glad to be blind-sided in my life."

Seth interrupted, poking a little fun at his own girlfriend in return. "I don't believe she was aware of our first date until the following day," he said. "Isn't that right, sweetheart?"

"That's right," she said. "How was I supposed to know you didn't take girls on canoe rides at camp all the time?"

"Or that Kerri was my sister, not my girlfriend?"

Amber laughed.

"What's this?" Adam asked. He didn't recall ever hearing about that.

"The first day I met Seth," Amber explained, "I saw him with Kerri, and I assumed she was his girlfriend. I tried hard to not be jealous of her for the next three days, but I wasn't very successful. So I was pleasantly surprised when he told me she was his sister, although I still didn't think I had much of a chance to do anything about it."

"But she was wrong," Seth said.

"And here you are two years later, engaged and everything," Adam said.

Amber glanced at Seth. "Yep. There are other fish in the sea, but I like this one."

"I should get going," Lauren said. "I need to change."

"See you guys," Adam said, stepping away and following her out the back door. But before he let her go, he said, "I'm sorry we got interrupted. Meet me back here after campfire, okay? I want to tell you something."

"Okay."

"And Angel?" he whispered.

"Yeah?"

"I really like you too."

***

Heading back to her cabin, Lauren wondered what Adam had to tell her. She was glad she had been honest and told him how she felt, and she hoped he was being completely honest too. She didn't have any reason to believe he wasn't, but she wasn't used to taking a chance on love, so she didn't have any idea if she was being realistic about this.

She had often thought about wanting a boyfriend. She had liked a lot of different guys since her early teen years. She had often felt overlooked and wished it could be different. Just last week she had felt that way. But now with Adam expressing an interest in her, showing her affection on Saturday evening, and continuing to be attentive, she found herself thinking, *What now? Am I ready for this? I have no clue what I'm doing!*

They ended up sitting next to each other at campfire, but it was a total coincidence. Normally she sat with the girls in her cabin, as did the other counselors, but after they had found seats and sang a couple of songs, Justin asked all the counselors to come up front and sit on the front benches he had reserved for them. He did it as an object lesson to help the campers remember God will always place people in front of them to follow their good example when they are seeking to know Him more and live the right way. He shared about people God had placed in his life and then asked the counselors to volunteer to share examples from their lives.

Lauren sat beside Adam because he had been in the back and was the last counselor to make it up front, and the only remaining seat on the front benches was beside her. Lauren did manage to focus on what Justin was saying and thought of people who had given her a good example to follow: her brother, her parents, youth leaders, and a few of her peers she admired—especially those she had met this summer.

The counselors remained in the front until campfire time ended. The campers were sent elsewhere to receive instructions for the night game, and they were asked to remain in place because they were going to be part of the opposition keeping the campers from reaching their goal for the game. After the rules had been explained to them, she and Adam were paired together to guard the same area. This time it was because they were sitting beside each other.

They were told to go to the front gate and guard the mailbox where some clues were hidden, quite a walk from where they were, giving them plenty of time to talk on the way.

"I guess God is in the mood to give us a lot of delightful moments today," Adam said. "All through Fireside I was praying I'd have a chance to tell you what was on my mind earlier. I didn't expect Him to answer me like this."

She smiled. They were completely alone with only bright stars shining overhead in the black sky. They each had their flashlights with them but had turned them off so they wouldn't be spotted by campers until they surprised them by "catching" them with a beam of light, forcing them to flee into the brush and find an alternate route to the mailbox besides the main road.

"So you had nothing to do with this?" she asked. "No inside scoop from Frodo about how to end up out here all alone with me for the next thirty minutes?"

"Believe it or not, no. I haven't been running into you during games all summer and never noticed, have I?" He laughed. "This is the second time today."

"No," she said, recalling the many times she had hoped to get paired with Adam during games, but it had been rare.

"I think maybe God is trying to tell us something," he said. "How about you?"

"Like what?" she asked.

"Like, He has more plans for us than one Saturday together."

"What kind of plans?" she probed further.

"Good plans," he said.

She laughed. Adam had this very adorable way of keeping her in suspense. "What kind of good plans, Mr. Lightyear?"

"What kind of good plans are you hoping for, Angel?"

"I asked you first."

"Are you always this curious?"

"Are you always this difficult?"

"Are you always this beautiful?"

"You can't even see me right now. It's pitch black out here."

"I have a good memory, and I'm not just talking about your appearance. You're beautiful through and through, Lauren."

She gave up on that question and moved on to one he had mentioned earlier. "What did you want to tell me?"

"When?"

"Now!" she laughed. "You wanted to meet me in the dining room again, remember?"

"This isn't the dining room."

She folded her arms and gave him a look of impatience she knew he couldn't see, so she decided to remain silent until he answered her question. He could play this game all night.

He laughed at her silent dramatics. She fought to keep a straight face. Leaning closer, he whispered his answer in her ear, sending shivers clear through her and reminding her of the way he had whispered sweet words to her on Saturday night.

"I wanted to tell you Saturday was the best day of my life and how I know you're the right girl for me instead of Kerri."

She waited for him to go on. He stepped back and spoke in his normal voice, but he remained close enough for her to begin to see his face in the darkness.

"I actually started liking Kerri last summer—about two weeks before the summer ended. I thought about her all year, and when she was here again this summer and I found out she was going to Lifegate, my hopes of something happening with her rose to an all-time high. They were crushed when I also found out she had a boyfriend back home, but then Amber restored them a bit when she told me Kerri wasn't totally certain about Dylan and they had agreed to see other people."

"You knew that?" she asked. Kerri had deliberately not let that be widely known so she could turn down guys she wasn't interested in without hurting their feelings.

"I knew that," he said. "And I thought about going to her, letting her know how I felt, and saying, 'Let's give it a chance. We don't have to tell anyone and blow your cover, and if it's not working for you after one or two dates, you can just tell me, and I'll let it go.'"

"But you never did?"

"No."

"Why not?"

"Because it wasn't something I wanted enough to go through with."

"What does that have to do with me?"

He found her hands, holding them loosely in his own. "I may have had my eyes on Kerri all summer, but I was content to leave it at that. But when I saw you: I wasn't. When you walked out of the laundry room on Saturday, I went after you. I didn't want to put it off. I didn't want to hope for some time with you in the future. I wanted it—right then. And I wanted it enough to go through with it."

She hadn't thought about it that way. "Why did you finally see me?"

"Because Kerri wasn't there to be a distraction, I guess."

"And now that she's back?"

"I see her the same as any other girl—except you. Please believe that and let me love you, Lauren. I want to love you."

She wanted to believe him, but was she being naive in thinking he could actually mean that? Was she trusting him with her heart too much, too soon? She had no experience with this.

"I'm scared, Adam," she whispered. "I'm not used to this."

"Spend this Saturday with me, and I'll get you more used to it."

"Just you and me?"

"Just you and me. All day. How about Silver Falls?"

Silver Falls was well known by the staff as a good spot for a romantic date. The suggestion thrilled her, but she had something else she wanted to ask him before saying yes. They heard voices and running feet coming their way on the gravel road, and Adam stepped away from her. They both had their flashlights

126

ready and waited for the right moment to shine them on the approaching campers.

After they had done so, and the boys ran into the woods, Adam turned back to her and said, "So what do you think? Will you go on a date with me, Angel?"

"Can I ask you something first?"

"Yes."

"I felt safe with you on Saturday when we were at the park. Can I expect the same at Silver Falls?"

"In a mostly secluded location, perfect for doing lots of kissing, you mean?"

"Yes. That's what I mean."

"You can trust me, Lauren," he said seriously. "But if you're not comfortable with that suggestion, we can go someplace else. I don't care where we go as long as I have the day with you."

"Can I think about it?"

"About spending the day with me, or about going to Silver Falls?"

"Silver Falls." She laughed. "I don't need to think about if I want to spend the day with you."

They heard more voices in the distance along with the other group who had reached the mailbox and were sneaking their way back around them. A steady stream of campers came their way, and they didn't have a chance to talk again until the game had ended and they were heading back.

"Have you dated a lot, Adam?" she asked.

"Not really," he said. "And no one seriously."

"How did Saturday compare to other dates you've had?"

"It didn't. My other dates have either been awkward and uncomfortable, or just your standard,

'Get something to eat—go to the movies or whatever', but nothing special. Nothing that made me feel what I felt with you."

"What did you feel?"

"Relaxed—myself—like I never wanted it to end."

She knew she had felt the same, and she still did. "You mean like how I feel right now?"

"That's what I mean," he sighed, looking up into the sky. "Thanks for the surprise date, God. We'll take it as a sign of your approval."

They walked in silence the remainder of the way back, but before they reached the doors of the meeting room, she whispered something to him. "You can take me to Silver Falls on Saturday."

"Are you sure?"

"Yes, I'm sure. If you're not going to be a boyfriend I can trust, I'd like to know that before I let myself fall in love with you."

Chapter Fourteen

Matt was quiet on the drive to Sandy on Wednesday morning, and Mandy remained equally so. When Matt was being talkative, which defined his personality under normal circumstances, she could talk almost as much as he did if it was just the two of them. But this week when he'd been quiet, she felt no need to break the silence with meaningless chatter. If she had something to say, she said it, but otherwise she was content to simply be with him and listen.

It had only been a week and a half since she had seen her family, but it seemed like longer. Seeing her grandmother's house come into view, where her family had moved earlier this year after her grandpa had died and left Grandma alone, Mandy reached over and took Matt's hand.

"You okay?" she asked.

"Yeah," he said. "The silence at home has been deafening this week, but in the car it's nice. Sorry I'm not very talkative."

"It's fine. I just want to make sure you're okay before we go inside. We can go someplace else for awhile if you need to."

He stopped the car along the curb in front of the house and leaned over to give her a brief but tender kiss. "I need you. I'm all right as long as you're with me."

They went inside, and her mom and grandmother were there. Dad and T.J. were on a job this morning but would be home sometime this afternoon. She and Matt were planning to stay through dinner unless Matt felt the need to get back to his family sooner.

She gave her mom a long hug. "Hi, Mama."

"Good to see you," she said.

"Good to be here," she replied.

Her mother released her and looked up at Matt. "Hello, Matt," she said in a concerned tone. "How are you?"

He stepped forward and hugged her also, hanging on longer than Mandy had ever seen him do before. "Amanda is taking good care of me," he said.

"I'm very sorry for your loss. If there's anything we can do—"

He laughed softly. "You've done quite enough with letting me invade Amanda's life. I don't know what I would have done without her."

Mandy stepped around Matt to hug her grandmother as she came into the foyer, and Grandma gave Matt a hug also, saying something that brought tears to everyone's eyes. "I bet Charlie's having a real good time showing Mark around up there, Matthew."

"I'm sure you're right," Matt said.

They went into the living room and sat on the couch. Her grandmother brought them something to drink, and her mom asked if they were hungry for lunch yet. They said yes, and she went to make them sandwiches.

Mandy snuggled into Matt's side and draped her arm across his waist, something she felt more comfortable doing here than at Matt's house. She wasn't sure what it was, but she got the feeling Matt's mother didn't approve of her, and she always felt uncomfortable showing Matt any kind of affection when she was around—like she was silently being accused of being too promiscuous with him. And the heightened emotions this week hadn't helped her feelings of self-consciousness around his mother.

But here she could be herself. Her parents had always been open and straightforward with her about not becoming sexually active before marriage, but they trusted her to make good choices about the time she and Matt spent together. Mandy felt like if she and Matt ever began to struggle with it, she would feel comfortable going to her mom and talking to her, but Matt had very high standards, and he hadn't wavered. She knew that was partially because he and Seth kept each other accountable to the times they spent with their girlfriends, as well as praying for each other and keeping each other on track spiritually.

"What are you thinking about?" she asked.

"That I love you."

She looked up at him and smiled. "And why are you thinking that right now?"

"Because this is the best I've felt all week. And all I have right now is you and your love, and that's all I need to get me through this."

Mandy spoke the words she meant with all of her heart. She hadn't known Matt for very long, and she had no idea how she had become such a vital part of his life, but that's exactly what she wanted to be.

"I love you, Matthew. And I'm here."

***

Colleen pulled the letters from her mailbox. The top one simply had her name on the outside of the envelope, and she knew it was from Blake. The middle one was from her mom, and the bottom one had foreign stamps on it and was from Chris.

He had written her a couple of times this summer from China where he'd been on an eight-week mission trip. His letters had been mostly informative about what they were doing and things she could pray for. Going to sit on one of the window-seats of the empty staff lounge, she decided to read his first and was not at all prepared for what he had to say. It was short and to the point.

Dear Colleen,

By the time you get this letter, I'll probably be back in Portland. My visa for staying in Vietnam fell through, and unless something happens in the next few days, I'm not going to be able to go there like I planned. I can probably go next year if I apply sooner, but maybe it's not meant to be. In a way I'm glad. I miss my family, and I miss you. Please call me when you get this.

Chris

Colleen stared at the letter for a long time. She had never considered the possibility of Chris coming home at the end of the summer instead of going to Vietnam like he'd planned. And she had to ask herself: *If I had known he was only going to be gone for two months, would we still be together?*

She knew she had to tell him about Blake, and she had every intention of doing so. She had moved on, and she was happy with her choice. But her heart ached for Chris. First he hadn't been able to go to Vietnam like he wanted, and now he would find out he had lost her as well.

"Hey."

Blake's voice and sudden presence startled her. They had agreed to meet at this time for her afternoon break like they had been doing all week, but her thoughts had been elsewhere for the last minute.

"Sorry, didn't mean to scare you," he said. "Didn't you hear me come in?"

"No," she said, passing the letter to him. "I just got this in the mail."

He read it over and looked at her. He had a panicked look on his face he was trying to hide, and she smiled.

"God really does answer our prayers, doesn't He?"

"You've been praying for Chris to come back early?"

"No," she said, taking the letter back from him. "Ever since Chris and I got back together last summer, I've been praying for God to guide our relationship and make it last if it was meant to be, or bring it to an end at the right time in a healthy way."

Blake didn't relax yet. She smiled at him and explained her thinking.

"If I had known Chris was only going to be gone for two months, I don't think I would have let him go. We were doing fine. We had a good relationship. And God had led us to go to the same college. But now I can see our relationship was only meant to be temporary. I'm not sure I would know that if I hadn't met you during a time when I could let something happen between us." She reached over and laid her hand on his. "This is what I want, Blake. I can't explain it, but I know."

"Are you going to call him?"

"Yes."

"Do you want to see him this weekend?"

"No. I want to go to the beach with you like we planned."

He gave her a tentative smile.

"Unless you're looking for a good excuse to get rid of me," she teased him. "I can pretend this changes everything between us if that's what you want."

"I hope you know the answer to that."

"I got another letter from someone else here," she said, setting the ones from Chris and her mom aside and holding up his. "May I read it now, or do you want me to wait?"

"You can read it," he said.

She took out the piece of notebook paper and began reading his words silently to herself:

Dear Colleen,

It's Wednesday morning and we just finished with the counselor meeting, and since I have some spare time before breakfast, I want to share some of my thoughts with you.

I think about you constantly. Even when I'm busy doing other things, you're there, just a thought away. Saturday was like a dream for me, and I'm still not sure it actually happened.

As you know, I've only had one other girlfriend, and I never had a day like that with her, even though we were together for five months. You are very special to me, Colleen, and I love everything about you. I love your smile—especially the way you smile at me. I love your eyes. They're so deep and expressive, and I think you are so beautiful. I love the way you make me feel. I love your kisses. Thank you for trusting me with such a special gift. And I love the person you are: intelligent and caring and open and honest. I don't need you to be anyone else for me other than who you already are.

I talked to my dad last night, and my parents are planning to go to Shasta Lake during that final week before Lauren and I leave for school. Would you like to come? I'd love to have you there, but if you can't, I understand. I know this year is going to be tough for us, or at least for me, but I never would have let this happen if I didn't think it would be worth it.

I love you, Colleen Tehya Garcia. You make me feel so alive. You make my heart feel warm and complete. I can't wait to kiss you and hold you in my arms again. Thanks for taking a chance with me. I hope you never regret it.

Blake

Colleen looked at him. He had a worried expression on his face, like he hoped he hadn't said too much. But she needed that kind of openness and honesty from him, especially now. Chris had never told her that he loved her, and she had never told him so either. Her time with Chris had always been more activity-related than emotionally close. He was a good friend—someone she trusted and could talk to, but he wasn't romantic or someone who would have written her a letter like that.

"Something tells me I'm not going to regret it," she said. "Not taking a chance with you when I did, now *that* I would have regretted. If I hadn't, I would be so confused right now because I would know I have feelings for you, but I'd be wondering if I should let things continue with Chris instead."

"What made you take that chance?"

"I couldn't put it off anymore. I'd been wanting it for weeks, but I kept telling myself I wasn't thinking rationally."

"What about Shasta Lake? You up for that?"

"Absolutely," she said. "Just this morning I was thinking about asking you if we could spend part of that week together. Are you sure your family won't mind?"

He smiled. "I talked to my dad for an hour, and mostly about you. They hadn't wanted to say too much until it was official between us, but they really like you and had been hoping it would work out."

"Really? Why? They barely know me."

"But they know me, and I'm sure they've never seen a girl make me smile the way you do."

Chapter Fifteen

On Thursday morning Seth had breakfast with his high school campers and left with Amber and Kerri for Portland at eight-thirty. The memorial service for Matt's brother was at eleven o'clock, and he wanted to be a little early so they would have a chance to talk to Matt beforehand. Seth had been there for his friend during several critical moments of his life over the past two years, but he knew none of those times compared to this. He was glad Mandy had been able to talk to him better than he could on Sunday, because he'd been out of words and had no idea how to help his friend face the tragic death of his little brother.

Other than his grandfather who had died when he was thirteen, Matt's brother was the closet person Seth had ever lost. He didn't know Mark well, but after being Matt's friend for five years, he had spent a fair amount of time with Mark when he had been at Matt's house, playing video games or whatever, and he had a difficult time believing Mark was actually gone.

He tried to imagine one of his siblings dying anytime soon, but he couldn't. He didn't want to think about losing Amber and tried not to go there. If he ever lost her in a tragic way, he knew she would be in

Heaven and he would join her there someday, but that wouldn't keep him from missing her tremendously and having to start his life over again. He didn't know exactly what the future held at this point, but after two years of having Amber in his life, he knew without a doubt he wanted her forever.

She had been a sweet surprise to him when he met her two years ago. He hadn't planned on dating or getting involved in a serious relationship until after high school and possibly not until after college. He had nothing against dating or falling in love, but he didn't think he was ready for it. Some of the guys in his life he looked up to had decided to delay dating, and he thought it was a good move. He knew the temptations at this age were very great. He had a difficult time looking at a beautiful girl without having thoughts about her he knew he shouldn't, and he couldn't imagine how much that would increase if he was actually alone with a girl he was attracted to and she wanted him to kiss her.

But then he met Amber, and she caught his eye immediately, but in a different kind of way. He saw her beautiful smile and face and well-shaped figure, but he also saw an inner beauty, especially up close when he looked into her captivating brown eyes. He wasn't sure what it was at the time, but he knew there was something different and special about her, and he wanted to discover what it was before that week at camp ended.

She often mentioned the disasters that had brought them together and made her unforgettable: She had spilled her Pepsi all over the floor at Taco Bell right after he met her; she had fallen flat on her face during a cabin skit; she tripped over a rock in the woods during a night-game and cut her leg, and he had found her, stopped the bleeding, and carried her to the nurse.

But the times he remembered most from that week weren't those moments. He remembered the first time he saw her at camp after meeting her in town initially: She was sitting in front of him at campfire on the second night, and he didn't realize it was her because she didn't have her hair in a ponytail like she had the day before. She had worn it long with a clip holding the sides away from her face, and she looked beautiful with the glow of the fire reflecting off her face. Her eyes were closed, and she was singing with a look of pure joy. He watched her almost the entire hour they were there, eventually realizing she was the girl from Taco Bell he had hoped to see again.

He had seen her other times she wasn't aware of also: at meals when she was seated a few tables away but was directly within his line of sight; at the volleyball tournament where her cabin played in the court adjacent to where his sister was playing; at every meeting and campfire he always knew exactly where she was sitting and watched her whenever possible; and he'd had fifteen minutes completely alone with her in the nurse's office after her accident when the nurse had asked him to stay and keep an eye on her while she went to talk to Amber's counselor and call her parents. She had been asleep the whole time, and he prayed the whole time, asking God why he felt so drawn to her and what he was supposed to do about it.

And there had been the times she was fully aware of but she didn't know how much his time with her affected him. He sat beside her at dinner one night and had gotten to know her as more than a beautiful girl who had captured his attention. She was easy to talk to. She had a wonderful laugh. She was funny and athletic and very kind and sweet to everyone around her. She was dressed simply in shorts and a t-shirt with her hair in a ponytail, and he thought she looked adorable.

He had gotten up the nerve to talk to her the following morning and see if she had plans that afternoon. He wanted to go for a walk with her or take her for a canoe ride, but her schedule was already full, so he suggested they could do something the following afternoon, and she seemed interested.

He couldn't figure out if she liked him or not. She was kind and sweet to him, but she didn't flirt in any obvious ways. He was a little afraid she saw him as an annoyance, and when he heard someone calling for help in the woods during the game and he discovered it was her, his immediate fear was she would think he was following her. But he hadn't been. He and his cabinmates just happened to be there, and as soon as he saw the blood gushing out of her leg, all he could think about was helping her and treating her as gently as possible. But she was in a lot of pain, and having to press on the cut to stop the bleeding had only brought her more. She had been cooperative and allowed him to do what needed to be done before he could carry her to the nurse and get bandaged up.

He was glad he hadn't had to do that part but could hold her hand and help distract her from the pain. It had been an emotional night where he went from saying to himself 'I think I like this girl,' to 'I think God is trying to tell me something, and I like what He's saying!' It took him another twenty-four hours to decide for certain he wanted to see her again after the week ended. He had been on his way there, but the canoe ride he took with her on Friday afternoon had clinched it for him.

She had told him things about her family, her life, her view of herself, and her relationship with God he suspected she didn't tell just anybody. She was insecure and yet courageous. She was close to her family and a few friends, but there was a loneliness in her heart he wanted to fill. She didn't see herself as anything special, but he thought she was amazing. She wasn't like other girls he knew. He saw her differently. And he liked what he saw. Physically, emotionally, and spiritually. She had a real relationship with God. He could see it. And he knew that had a lot to do with her joy and light that had caught his attention in the first place.

They had been through some difficult moments together in the last two years, but mostly related to those around them, not with each other. They didn't fight—ever. He knew they disappointed each other from time to time, but nothing major. He couldn't stand the thought of her being angry with him, and he constantly made sure things were right between them. He could usually tell if she had been hurt or felt uncomfortable by something he said or did, and he hated it when that happened. She could be tough when it came to physical pain, but emotionally she was more fragile, and he loved that about her.

She had been strong this week. Stronger than him. And he needed that right now. When he knew how to help his friends, he was fine. He could tell Matt what he thought about his negative choices. He could tell him to stop being an idiot, get on-track with God, and make the decisions he already knew were right. But telling him how to feel when his only brother had been killed in a senseless accident and he felt responsible? He didn't know how to handle that.

Give me the words, Jesus. And if I shouldn't say anything, help me to keep my mouth shut. I want to help, but I'm not sure I can. May I be whatever he needs me to be.

***

Mandy waited upstairs in Matt's room until his parents left the house. Matt had told them he wanted to drive his own car to the church rather than having them all ride together. He wanted the option to leave before them and go somewhere with his friends who were coming today, but it had caused an all-out war between him and his parents. Tensions had been high since last night when they returned from visiting her family. They had arrived an hour later than they said because Matt wanted to stop by Mark's best friend's house to see how he was doing, and they had ended up staying longer than Matt expected.

His dad had yelled at him for being late, as if they'd come back at two o'clock in the morning instead of nine-thirty, and he was fourteen instead of eighteen. Mandy knew his mom was upset they had left at all, and she felt bad, but she knew Matt had needed to get away.

They'd had a great day, and Mandy didn't understand why his parents were being so hard on him. He had been the model son all week. He had been stronger than they had. He loved his family and hated what had happened, but they were acting like it was the opposite.

When she saw them get into their car and drive away, she took her purse from the bed and headed out of the room. Matt was sitting on the couch in the family room, crying like she hadn't heard him do since Sunday afternoon. Sitting beside him, she let him cry and gently stroked his hair.

"I don't want to go," he said. "We look like this perfect family to everyone else, but we're not. I'm messed up. They're messed up. Mark was messed up. I'm tired of pretending."

"Pretending what?"

He sighed and sat back. She didn't think he was going to answer her, but he did.

"I didn't realize it until this week, but my parents have no faith. They talk about it. They teach about it. But they don't live it. When we went to put that cross by the road, I tried telling them about Mark being in Heaven and how we shouldn't act like he isn't, and my dad slapped me in the face and told me not to upset my mother more than she already was; and then last night after you went to bed, I went back downstairs to make peace with them after the big shouting match we had, and they told me I needed to break up with you because I was going to end up disgracing our family more by getting you pregnant.

"And I said, 'I can't get her pregnant when we're not even having sex,' and my dad said, 'One of these days you will. We know you, Matt. You're going to mess up her life just like you messed up your brother's."

"Oh, Matt," she said, her heart absolutely breaking for him. He hadn't been blaming himself all week, but his dad's words had brought all of those feelings back.

"I admitted I've made mistakes in the past but I've surrendered my life to God and am walking a different path now, and he said, 'Yeah, we'll see how long that lasts.' They talk about Jesus changing lives—my dad is the pastor of evangelism for crying out loud, but he doesn't believe Jesus can change *my* life? What kind of faith is that?"

"They're just upset, Matthew—"

"No, I don't think that's it. I think this is who they really are deep down, and this is bringing it all to the surface. I can say that because I was the exact same way on Sunday before you came and said that to me about Mark being in Heaven. I knew that in my head. I've been taught it since I was a little kid, and I've been teaching it to kids all summer. But when it came to losing my brother, I realized I hadn't let the reality of Heaven and what Jesus has done to get us all there reach my heart. I don't know, maybe my dad's right. I'm saying I've changed, but maybe I really haven't. Maybe I'm just pretending."

"I don't believe that," she said. "I haven't been dating a pretender, Matthew. I see the real you, and you're genuine. You're not perfect, but you're not afraid to admit it either. And you know what real love is. I know because you show it to me all the time."

146

Once again her words seemed to penetrate his heart, and she felt his body relax as he took her into his arms and accepted the truth the way she saw it. And she honestly believed what she was saying.

"Please don't make me go," he said. "I don't want to. I can't."

"I won't make you do anything you don't want to do, Matt. But don't let the last thirty minutes determine what you do today. If you don't go because of that, you might always regret it."

"We have some time," he sighed. "I think I'll go up to Mark's room. Is it okay if I go alone?"

"Yes."

"Thank you, Amanda. For being who you are. For being here. For everything." He kissed her in a needy way. It was a dangerous kiss because she liked the way it made her feel, they were alone in the house, and Matt was emotionally vulnerable. But she knew it wasn't the right way to deal with his confusion and pain.

"Go," she said, pushing him gently away from her. "I'll wait."

"Come with me," he tempted her.

"Not a good idea," she said. "If you want to stay home, that's fine, but we're not staying here to do that."

Chapter Sixteen

When Seth arrived at the church along with Amber and his sister, he looked around for Matt but didn't see him or Mandy anywhere. Matt's parents were in the foyer, greeting everyone as they arrived and thanking them for coming. Seth hugged them both sincerely and expressed his sympathy for their loss. He expected one of them to say where Matt was, but when neither of them did, he asked. It was too big of a church to have to go searching for him.

"I don't think he's here yet," his dad said, seeming a bit agitated. Seth hadn't talked to Matt since Tuesday, so he wondered if something had happened since then to send Matt back into his protective shell.

Stepping back outside with Amber, he decided to call him. He tried his cell phone but only got his voice mail, and no one answered at the house. They waited outside for him to arrive. Seth saw quite a few people he knew while they were standing there, especially students who either knew Matt or Mark well. Several others asked him where Matt was, and he had to tell them he wasn't sure.

It was a strange role for him. He normally kept close tabs on his best friend. To not know where he was or how he was doing made him realize things were changing between them. Not in a bad way, but a natural one with both of them having serious relationships that were becoming deeper and more of a priority to them than the friendship they had with each other. He relaxed a bit at the thought of him being with Mandy. Wherever they were, he knew she was being everything he needed her to be.

His only concern was that something had happened between them, and Matt not being here was more about losing her than his brother. Seth had never seen Matt like when he was with Mandy. He wasn't just dating her. He didn't just have a fun time with her. He was falling in love with her. Something he had experienced himself with Amber from the beginning of their relationship until now, and he knew losing Mandy would absolutely devastate Matt at this point.

He felt relieved when he saw them coming toward the front steps of the church, walking hand in hand and seeming their usual selves—as much as could be expected today.

"Everything all right?" he asked. The service was scheduled to begin in five minutes.

"I'm all right," Matt said. "I needed some time at home before I had to face this."

The four of them went inside, and Matt joined his family in walking to the front of the church where seats had been reserved for them. Matt asked Mandy, as well as him and Amber, to come with him, and they did.

The service was a mixture of sadness for Mark's absence and joy for the good memories he had left behind. Mark had been a popular kid with many friends, talents, ambitions, and qualities. The tragedy surrounding his death was mentioned, but the focus remained on other things. He would be missed. He had impacted others' lives in good ways. His life had been cut short, but it had counted for something. He wasn't gone, just in a different place. Seth had a constant lump in his throat, but he smiled and laughed at the appropriate times. Mark's death was a reminder to live each day to the full and be thankful for all he had.

The only one who didn't cry in their row was Matt, but he didn't look withdrawn and in shock like he had on Sunday. He was at peace. Several times he looked at Mandy and gave her a peaceful smile, even when tears were streaming down her cheeks. If Seth didn't know better, he would have thought Mandy had been the one to lose her brother and Matt was being her supportive boyfriend, but somehow Mandy's tears were comforting him, and Seth accepted an obvious reality he told Matt afterwards when he had a moment alone with him while Amber and Mandy went to the ladies' room together.

"She's taking you officially off my hands, isn't she?"

"Amanda?"

"Yes. How does it feel to have a beautiful girl as your best friend instead of me?"

He smiled. "Pretty great. No offense, Seth, but she's definitely the one person I needed most this week."

"None taken. I'm sure I'd say the same thing about Amber if it was me going through this."

"But without you, man, I never would have gotten her in the first place."

Seth knew what he meant. And he knew Matt wasn't talking about the fact he and Amber had done a little creative planning to get him some time with Mandy last spring. He was talking about the times he had talked to him about getting his life straight with God, to stop making stupid choices, and being the best friend he knew how to be. It had been a tough road, one he often hadn't wanted to be on with his troubled and misguided friend, but he had traveled it with him, and he couldn't be happier now. He would gladly pass the title of being Matt's best friend to Mandy, but he wasn't going to completely remove himself from his life either.

Now that Matt had Mandy, Seth was planning to make sure he did everything possible to keep her, but he knew right now wasn't the time for any of his blunt questions about all of that. Today Matt was grieving the loss of his brother, and he was here to support him.

"What's with the look I see on your face today?"

"What look is that?" Matt asked.

"Peaceful, with a bit of joy mixed in. It's not the look you had when we left here on Sunday. And I'm not sure I've ever seen it—even when everything has been fine."

Someone interrupted them to tell Matt how sorry she was. It was his former girlfriend, Clarissa, and Matt accepted her sorrow-filled words graciously and thanked her for coming. She hugged him, and he received the affectionate display as he would with anyone else. When Clarissa released him, he asked how she was doing. They hadn't seen one another since graduation, and they stood there talking until Mandy and Amber returned.

Matt saw them coming and slipped his arm around Mandy as soon as she reached his side. She seemed indifferent to the person Matt was talking to, and Seth supposed Mandy didn't know who she was. Matt didn't introduce them, and Clarissa stepped away after another expression of sympathy.

"I'm very sorry, Matt. You and your family are in my prayers," she said, giving him a brief kiss on the cheek and then turning away.

***

Matt watched Clarissa leave, and he had an overwhelming sense of gratitude and love for his Savior. Jesus had rescued him from one of the biggest mistakes he could have ever made. And not only had He gotten him away from Clarissa, but He had also begun to prepare him for meeting the girl he was really meant to be with.

He didn't deserve Amanda, and he knew it. But Jesus had given her to him anyway, and the thought made tears fill his eyes and drip onto his cheeks for the first time since letting out all of his tears for Mark before they left the house.

He had been grieving for his brother all week, but he felt ready to leave the mourning behind and go on, celebrating the wonderful life available to him if he let Jesus lead him. Amanda, his other friends, the ministries he could be a part of, and whatever great plans God had in store for his future: He wanted to embrace all of it and live the abundant life Jesus had for him, even in the midst of the sorrow and pain he was currently experiencing. He missed his brother deeply, and he knew he would for a long time—for the rest of his life in varying degrees. But he also knew God promised to work all things together for good, and he believed that with all of his heart.

He had to. If he let go of hope, he had nothing, and he couldn't function that way. He may as well be dead himself if he wasn't going to expect good and wonderful things to come from the God who loved him. Even in his sorrow, he felt the presence of Jesus like never before, and he knew he wanted that more than anything. Even more than Amanda and his own family and his other friends. He needed to embrace God's love for him and live in the reality of it every day.

"Let's go do something," he said to the three friends surrounding him.

"All of us?" Seth asked.

"Yes, and Kerri too. Where is she?"

"Around here somewhere. I'll go find her and meet you at the car. It's just up the street, much closer than yours, I'm sure."

"I'm sure you're right," Matt said, beginning to lead Amanda toward a side door of the church. He knew they would never get out of here if they tried to leave through the front.

"Are you sure you're all right?" Amanda asked him once they were outside and heading up the downtown street toward Seth's car. "It's okay to cry, Matthew. We'll all let you do that if you need to."

He didn't respond until they reached Seth's car. He wasn't sure he could express what he was feeling right now. God was pouring joy into his heart. Hope and joy. Not just to help him deal with the loss of his brother, but to help him deal with life. The things here now, and those he would be facing tomorrow, and the day after that. There was so much to experience and learn and enjoy. Good things. Worthwhile things. Things that mattered and made a difference.

He started with the person right in front of him, kissing her tenderly for several moments, not caring who was watching or what they were thinking as they walked by.

"Do you know who that girl was?" he asked. "The one I was talking to when you and Amber came back?"

"No. Who?"

"Clarissa."

She knew the name because he had talked about her a lot when they first started dating. He had wanted her to know where he'd been and how different he wanted their relationship to be from what he and Clarissa had. They hadn't ever actually had sex but had come dangerously close a few times, and their relationship had been unhealthy in other ways too.

He had never even liked her all that much. She was pushy and manipulative and was never happy unless she got her way. But he had dated her because she was beautiful and turned him on, and because all of his friends gave him credit for having a girl like her to go out with, and make out with, whenever they had the chance. All of his friends except Seth.

Amanda didn't respond to the news of seeing Clarissa, but he could read her thoughts. They were written all over her face. And her reaction was exactly what he expected and the reason he had mentioned it. He wanted Amanda to understand something and believe it with all of her heart. He wanted it more than anything he could ever want for himself.

He touched her cheek with his fingertips and held her face in his palm. Leaning down and kissing her gently, with sincere and pure passion, he told her what he had been thinking ever since Clarissa had turned away from him.

"You're the most special person in my life, Amanda. I am so thankful for you. Please believe that. Just like I need to believe Mark is in Heaven to get me through this, you need to believe I need you and love you. If you want to walk away from me at some point for some other reason, fine, but don't let a lack of belief in my love for you be the reason, okay?"

She nodded but didn't speak, and he kissed her again, lingering until they were interrupted by Seth's teasing words.

"All right, Matthew Abramson. You're drawing a crowd. We'll have to start selling tickets soon."

He smiled but didn't distance himself from the beautiful girl in his arms. "Where's Kerri?" he asked, seeing she wasn't with them.

"We found her with Dylan. She invited him to come along with us, but he was parked the other way, so I'm going to call her when we decide what we're doing, and they'll meet us there."

Seth opened the door for Amber and went around to the driver's side. Matt opened the back door and let

Amanda get in first. She scooted over to the other side, and he got in beside her.

"So where to, Spider-boy?" Seth asked.

Matt didn't have to think about it. Mark's favorite place to go before he had started getting into trouble was the skate park near their house. He had overheard a couple of Mark's friends saying they were planning to go there this afternoon, and Matt knew if there were skate parks in Heaven, that's where his brother would be.

Chapter Seventeen

Kerri walked with Dylan to his car. He opened the door for her, and she slipped inside. She had met him inside the church after they arrived, agreed to sit with him during the service, and had remained by his side afterwards, talking with him quietly and with others they passed. She hadn't asked him the question foremost on her mind yet. It hadn't seemed appropriate inside.

He started the car and turned on the AC, waiting for Seth to call and let them know where they were going. She decided this was her best window of opportunity since they were alone.

"Did you call Janelle this week?"

"Yes," he said.

She laughed when he didn't elaborate. "And?"

"I'm going to see her tomorrow."

"In Seattle?"

"Yep."

"To meet her family?"

"Yes."

"What did she say when you called her?"

He laughed. "Aren't you the nosy ex-girlfriend?"

"Dylan! I'm not just your ex-girlfriend, I'm your friend, and if I'm going to let you go to be with this other girl, I want to make sure she's worthy of you."

He smiled. "All right. We talked for two hours after I told her what happened with you and me."

"Two hours? I'm not sure you ever spent two hours talking with me face-to-face! Okay, now I'm jealous. I changed my mind. I had you first."

He smiled at her teasing and sighed. A happy sigh she hadn't seen out of him before. It was almost like he was a different person. He hadn't even cut his hair yet.

"Okay, spare me the two-hour version. What did she say when you told her about us? That's all I want to know and then I'll leave you alone."

"The last time I saw her, I told her I would call her either way to let her know. So when I called, I said, 'Kerri didn't meet anyone else, and at first I was happy because I didn't think I wanted to lose her. But as the day went on, I kept thinking about you and ended up mentioning you one too many times. When she discovered I'd met someone else, she told me she was letting me go.' And Janelle said, 'What's that mean?' And I said, 'It means, I think I'm in love with you, and I couldn't hide that from her, even with as much as I thought I wanted to.'"

Kerri was in shock. Dylan was one of the most reserved and cautious guys she had ever met. He had pursued and courted her for several months, only kissed her a few times, and never came close to saying he was in love with her.

"All right," she said, knowing without a doubt he was officially out of her life and she had made the right decision. "Invite me to the wedding, Dylan Jacobsen."

***

"Do you want to stop at your house and get your board?" Seth asked.

"It's in my car," Matt said. "We can pick it up on the way."

Matt directed him to where he had parked, and Seth asked him something before he got out of the back. "Do you want to drive over and meet us there?"

"And miss the opportunity to snuggle with my girl? No way."

Matt hopped out and Mandy smiled. Seth turned back to look at her and said, "He is so in love with you. I hope you know that."

"I do," she said, feeling ready to accept that reality more than ever. She couldn't get the image of Clarissa out of her head. She hadn't thought much of it when she had seen the beautiful girl talking to Matt, supposing she was someone he knew from church expressing her sympathy for his loss, but she had made the mental observation the girl was very pretty. Clarissa was the image of someone she usually envied for her beautiful hair and facial features and a body that looked like something right out of a fashion magazine.

But that wasn't what Matt wanted. He'd had it once, but he walked away. He wanted her: plain ol' Amanda Elizabeth Smith, and not only did he want her, he loved her for exactly who she was, and he thought *she* was beautiful!

For the remainder of the day, Mandy let Matt grieve in his own way, like she had been doing all week. She didn't tell him to cry or not cry, to laugh or not laugh. She watched him do tricks on his skateboard with Mark's friends, and when he came to sit beside her and watch, she welcomed his displays of affection and sweet words—some said for all to hear and others for her ears only.

"I want to go back to camp tomorrow," he said when Seth asked him if he planned to return to get his stuff at some point. "I'm going to talk to Dave about speaking at Fireside tomorrow night."

"About Mark?"

"Yes. Did you know he was supposed to be there this week?"

"I thought so," Seth said. "But I wasn't sure."

"He was, and I want to share that with the high schoolers who are there this week, let them know about the bad choices he was making that cost him his life, but also share the hope we have this isn't the end."

"That's great, man," Seth said. "Dave actually asked me if I would share something about it, but I wanted to ask you first."

Matt turned and put his arm around her. "Now why doesn't that surprise me?"

Mandy smiled and gave him a hug. "I'm so proud of you," she whispered. "I love you."

"I love you," he said. "Will you go with me?"

"Yes."

They had dinner with Seth, Amber, Kerri, and Dylan. Mandy had heard from Amber that Kerri and Dylan had decided to not continue seeing each other, and she thought it was nice they could still be friends. She and Matt returned to his house, and Matt wasn't looking forward to facing his parents. They hadn't talked at the memorial service, and he had let them know earlier he would likely spend the afternoon with his friends rather than going to the family dinner they were having at the house, but he knew they weren't happy about it, and he also knew they wouldn't be thrilled about him going back to camp tomorrow.

"I want to respect them, Amanda, but I don't want them to drag me into their unhealthy grief. I can't go there. It suffocates me."

"No matter what you face in there, Jesus is with you, Matthew. Just believe in His love and trust Him to uphold you. That's all He expects from you."

He held her close in the evening quietness of the neighborhood. It had been a warm day, but it was nice right now, and she prayed silently for Matt, for their relationship, and for his relationship with his parents; and she knew he was doing the same.

***

"How is he?" Blake asked.

"Okay," Seth replied. "He's coming tomorrow."

Seth went on to explain why, and Blake wasn't too surprised Matt wanted to share about Mark, but he was a little surprised he would be ready this soon. Blake could talk about his younger brother's tragic death now, but it had taken him years to get to that point.

"You think he's ready for that?"

"As far as I could tell. Tomorrow may prove otherwise, but I think we should give him the freedom if that's what he wants."

Blake agreed and said he would tell Dave about it tomorrow. He could hear the camp bell ringing and knew the night game was over and the campers would be heading for the cabins in about ten minutes. He decided to ask Seth something on a different subject. They had a few minutes to spare and no one else was around. Seth had come to his room to let him know they were back.

"How did you manage to date a girl for two years, be away from her the majority of that time, and end up engaged to her?"

Seth smiled. "I have no idea."

Blake laughed, but he was honestly looking for practical advice. "Come on, Nemo. Help me out."

Seth thought for a moment and then responded seriously. "I think it was several things. Number one, we both clung to God, and I think that helped us to cling to each other. We kept our relationship healthy and pure, not just physically but also emotionally. I can usually tell when something is bothering Amber, and I never let that stuff slide. I'm very aggressive about always making sure things are right between us, not assuming it because she doesn't say something directly."

"What do you think went wrong between Colleen and Chris?"

"I don't think anything went wrong, it just wasn't meant to be. And to tell you the truth, I wasn't that surprised when they broke up. Chris was excited about it in the beginning, but I saw him lose that as

164

time went by. Chris tried to fit Colleen into his schedule instead of making her the priority and fitting everything else around her."

"Do you think it would be a mistake for me to go to Lifegate this year? I could take a year off, or transfer to Multnomah."

"Have you talked to Colleen about that?"

"No."

"I don't think it would be a mistake unless you feel God leading you to move to Portland."

"How am I supposed to know? I have two weeks to decide."

"You get close to God, Blake. As close as you can, and you listen. He will tell you. That's how I knew I was supposed to go to Amber's birthday party two years ago, and to ask her to marry me last month."

$$* * *$$

"Did you call Chris today?" Amber asked Colleen as they walked toward the girls' cabin area to get themselves and their hyper high school campers into bed for the night.

"Yes."

"What did you say?"

"That I'm seeing someone else."

"How did he take it?"

"I'm not sure. He said he understood and had been expecting me to possibly say I didn't want to get back together, but I don't think he was prepared for that to be my reason."

"Are you still feeling sure about Blake being the right one for you?"

"I've had a few moments where I've thought, 'But I thought Chris was the right one too.' But every time I see Blake, all of that goes away."

"Like right now, you mean?" she said, seeing Blake and Seth coming from the housing area where Blake and the other senior staff members lived.

Colleen smiled. "Like right now," she said.

They both slowed their stride and waited for Blake and Seth to cross their path. Amber had seen Seth ten minutes ago, and spent the entire day with him, but she was still thrilled by a few seconds of being near him. Mark's memorial service today had reminded her of how short life can be, and she hoped to have Seth in her life for a good long time, but there were no guarantees, and she wanted to cherish every moment she had with him.

She felt she had done that over the last two years. It had been difficult to be away from him while they were living an hour away from each other, but she knew it had made their time together that much sweeter. She was really looking forward to going to college with him in two more weeks though.

He gave her a sweet smile and said a simple, 'Hi, sweetheart. Sweet dreams,' as he gave her a brief hug. He had always called her that, and she loved it. Getting to know him and being completely comfortable with him had taken time, but she had always known he cared about her.

In some ways she couldn't believe they were engaged. It seemed perfectly natural and unbelievable at the same time. In a million years she never would have imagined getting engaged before her eighteenth birthday coming up at the end of the month. When she and Seth had been dating, she had never felt a strong need or desire to get married so young.

She had imagined them going to college and possibly getting married after graduation. Physically speaking, she knew it might be difficult to wait. Purity had always been at the core of their relationship, and she didn't want that to change. But when she began to think about marrying him sooner, it wasn't physical desire that led her to want to marry him. It was an emotional and spiritual desire to have a completeness to their relationship.

As she had prayed about it, talked with Seth and her parents about the possibility, and when Seth got down on one knee and proposed to her last month, she had been fully at peace with telling him yes. Since then their relationship had remained the same in some ways, but jumped to a completely different level in others. Especially in the security she felt in their relationship.

For a long time she had been worried about it all coming to a heartbreaking end, but she didn't feel that way anymore. If she knew one thing about Seth Kirkwood, she knew he took their engagement as seriously as marriage itself, and the only way he was going to walk out of her life was if she pushed him out of it, and she had absolutely no intention or desire to do that.

She loved him very much, and she needed him. She had a lot of good friends and a loving family, but no one in her life compared to the way Seth touched her heart. Physically, emotionally, and spiritually, he was exactly what she needed.

***

Matt entered the house behind Mandy and gave her a brief kiss before she headed upstairs. They had both agreed it might be better if she left him to face his parents alone. Walking to the formal living room where he heard voices, he expected to see more people than his mom and dad. Several cars were parked out front, and a smile came to his face when he saw his youth pastor was among the small crowd.

Standing outside with Mandy, he had been praying for guidance concerning his relationship with his parents and also for what he should do in the coming weeks. As much as he wanted to escape, go back to camp tomorrow, and head off to college in two weeks, he knew that might not be the right solution. He didn't feel their negative view of him right now was justified, but he did love them and knew he had caused them pain in the past, and he wanted to make things right as much as possible.

His mom stood to greet him, and he met her in the middle of the room with a hug. He held her gently and didn't say anything. He had always gotten along better with his mom during his rebellious days. His dad was busy most of the time and hadn't been there for him to talk to when he needed that. He had opened up to his mom more, especially during the last six months, but she couldn't always relate to the struggles and insecurities he felt as a boy on the brink of the adult world.

Some of his aunts and uncles were here along with his grandparents on his mom's side. They lived in California and had come up earlier in the week and were planning to stay until Sunday. His other grandparents lived nearby and had come by several times, but they weren't here currently.

His mom asked where Mandy was, and he told her she had gone upstairs. Other than that, nobody asked him any questions or talked to him directly. Matt didn't know if the mood of the room had been somber and quiet before he arrived, or if his presence had initiated it, but after a few minutes he made a casual exit and headed for the kitchen.

He silently hoped Pastor John would follow him, and after pouring himself some orange juice, he turned toward the approaching footsteps and welcomed him easily.

"You doing all right?" Pastor John asked, giving him a heartfelt hug that he had certainly been on the receiving end of before.

Despite all of his mistakes and failures, Pastor John had always been the same way with him—patient. He had never been afraid to tell him when he was heading down the wrong path, but he had never given up on him or been anything less than a perfect model of the forgiveness of God. Matt had learned more about God's grace through this man's actions toward him than from any message he had ever preached.

"I'm all right," he said. "You haven't been waiting around all afternoon for me, have you?"

"No. I just got here twenty minutes ago."

Matt took his juice from the counter and turned toward the back door. "Can we talk?" he asked.

"Absolutely," Pastor John said, following him out the door onto the deck. He closed the door behind them and waited for him to speak.

"What have you heard from Mom and Dad about me?"

He smiled. "That you've completely withdrawn from them, you almost didn't go to the memorial service today, and they've given up trying to understand and reach you."

"Wow. I didn't expect it to be that bad."

"What's the story, Matt? I'm listening and I'll believe whatever you say."

It wasn't the first time he had heard those words from his loving mentor, and Matt had usually been honest with him. It had always been difficult for him to lie to this man when confronted directly, and this time he didn't have anything to hide, but he knew he needed to be blunt and say things how he saw them.

"My parents don't like Amanda. They don't like that she's here, but I need her to be. If it wasn't for her, I would still be sitting up there in Mark's room not letting anybody in."

"Do they have any reason to not like her?"

Matt laughed. "Not unless being the kindest, sweetest, most loving and emotionally stable girl I've dated isn't the kind of girl they want for me."

"They're scared, Matt. One of their sons was killed because he had been drinking at a party they didn't know about, and their other son's track-record has some serious blemishes. Add a pregnant girlfriend to that, and their days of ministry could be over. People who can't manage their own children shouldn't be given the responsibility of leading anybody else. At least that's the way they see it."

The thought of his parents seeing Mandy that way absolutely broke his heart. He knew it wasn't because of her. They saw her that way because of his mistakes. No decent, upstanding Christian girl would ever be dating him unless she had her own indiscretions to hide.

He started to cry, and Pastor John's arms were there for him to fall into or he may have collapsed to the ground. He had no strength left. He had been so optimistic about his life and future all day, but maybe he was just fooling himself.

Maybe he couldn't have a girl like Amanda. Maybe he could never be who she would need him to be. And if he couldn't, he would prefer to let her go and not mess up her life too.

Chapter Eighteen

Lauren turned off the light and snuggled underneath her blankets. Normally when she went to bed this late, she fell asleep right away, but tonight sleep eluded her, and she knew why. She didn't know Matt well, but he had been on her mind a lot today. She had prayed for him several times and did so once again, but thoughts of him brought back the memories of her own brother's tragic death.

She had been trying to shut them out all week. She didn't have the time to dwell on the events of the past and how much she missed Kurt. But the horrific images of her brother's lifeless body, and the feelings of guilt, fear, and an incomparable pain flooded her thoughts in the quietness of the cabin, and she fought back the tears.

Why God? Why Kurt? Why Mark? You could have stopped it. Why didn't you?

She had been asking that question for five years and had come to have peace without a definite answer, knowing Kurt was in Heaven and believing God had His reasons, but right now that peace and trust was gone. She wanted her little brother to still be here. She wanted Matt to still have Mark. It all seemed so unfair and senseless.

Knowing she would never get to sleep if she didn't, Lauren whispered a prayer she had cried out in similar moments before. She never thought it would make a difference. She was too deep in despair and unbelief to get out anytime soon, but she was always wrong, so she did it anyway.

"I call as my heart grows faint; Lead me to the rock that is higher than I." It was from Psalm 61. Her pastor had directed her to the prayer the same day she'd had the dream about Kurt being in Heaven. That night He had given her a dream she was convinced was real. Other times He had simply given her peace or joy or a different way of looking at a difficult circumstance. But tonight He gave her something that lifted her out of the pit so fast, she almost felt guilty her mournful thoughts could flee so quickly.

God directed her thoughts to Adam. To the fun time they'd had together last weekend, his sweet kisses by the river, and the brief but delightful encounters they'd had throughout the week. She was looking forward to Saturday. She had some fears about not knowing how to act while spending a full day with him, but they didn't cloud her happy thoughts. She fell asleep with a smile on her face and the memory of Adam's soft, sweet lips on her own.

***

Mandy heard the bedroom door open behind her and turned from the window. She had left it open a bit so Matt wouldn't think she had gone to bed. She didn't especially need more time with him today, but she wanted to be here for him if he needed to talk or just be with her.

He closed the door behind him, which surprised her because he had been really careful this week about not giving his parents the wrong impression of their relationship. They hadn't been alone in his bedroom unless the door was open, and he only closed it when they were in Mark's room if he had something to talk to her about he didn't want his parents to overhear.

He crossed the room and came to her, slipping his arms around her waist and holding her close for a long time without saying anything. He'd done that often this week, but she sensed something different this time.

"What is it, Matthew?"

"I love you," he said.

Her response came easily. "I love you too."

"Why?" he asked.

"Because I do."

He sighed and stepped back to look into her eyes. Taking her hands firmly in his, he started to say something but started crying instead. "I never thought—" he began but couldn't finish.

She released one of his hands, reaching up to touch his tear-streaked cheek. "You never thought what?"

He regrasped her fingers and kissed them. "I never thought it would be like this."

"Be like what?"

"Feeling what I feel for you—like I can't let go and I can't hang on at the same time."

"Why not?"

"Because you deserve better, Amanda."

Oh, Matt. Not this again. "Better? Better than you?"

He stepped away from her.

She let him have a moment alone with his thoughts as he stared out the window before she took his hand and waited for him to look at her.

"You can think that all you want, Matthew, but it doesn't make it true."

He didn't respond, and she changed the subject.

"How did things go down there?"

"I spent more time talking to Pastor John than anyone."

"And was he the one who told you I deserve better?"

"Nobody has to tell me that, Amanda."

"Well, somebody needs to tell me!" She laughed, wrapping her arms around his waist and falling into him, knocking him off balance. He didn't fall, but it forced him to put his arms around her once again, and this time he didn't let go.

Matt held her in his strong but gentle arms for a long time, and it reminded her of when he had done the same at the beach last weekend. A lot had changed this week, and they had grown closer with each passing day, but the love in her heart for him was the same.

Her phone rang and she stepped away to see who was calling. It was Jenn, and she answered. She hadn't talked to anyone from camp all week, except Isaac to keep him updated on how Matt was doing.

Matt stepped out of the room, saying he would be back in a minute. Jenn wanted to know how things were going and if she was planning to go on the staff retreat this weekend.

"I haven't decided yet," she said. "I was going to talk to Matt about it tomorrow."

"You should bring him along."

She hadn't thought of that. "Do you think Isaac would mind?"

"I doubt it. He's had us pray for him at the counselor meeting every morning this week. How is he?"

"Okay. Today was the memorial service."

"Is there anything special you want me to pray for?"

She thought about that. What did Matt need most right now? What did she need? One week ago her life had seemed so in order, all planned out, nothing to worry about; but now nothing was certain. If Matt allowed his past mistakes to drag him down, he could push her away, never allowing himself to open up to her again. She felt uncertain about her plans for college, and even though Matt hadn't said anything, she could imagine leaving for California in two weeks being a difficult thing for him to do. He didn't know what he was doing next week, and neither did she.

"Cloud by day, fire by night," she said.

Jenn knew what she meant. That had been their staff theme for the summer. It was a reference to when the Israelites had followed the cloud during the day and the pillar of fire at night, showing them the way to travel through the desert. Throughout the summer it had been a reminder to her she could trust

God to guide her as a counselor each day; but now she didn't feel she *could* trust God, but that she *must*. She had no other option. Tomorrow they were going to Camp Laughing Water for the day. Beyond that, she had no clue.

"You've got it, sweetheart," Jenn said. "I need to go but just wanted to let you know we're all thinking of you and hoping to see you."

"Okay, thanks for calling," she said.

"See you when I see you."

Matt came back into the room as she clicked off the phone. He closed the door again and came to sit beside her on the bed, asking if everything was okay.

"That was Jenn. She's wondering if I'm coming on Saturday."

"Are you?" he asked.

"I don't know. What do you think?"

"What do I think about what?"

"If I'm going on the retreat or not."

"That's up to you, Amanda. If you want to go, it's fine."

She smiled at him. "But what do you think about it?" she repeated. "What do you want me to do?"

"Whatever you want," he said, but she didn't believe him.

"So if I went, you wouldn't miss me?"

He smiled. "I didn't say that."

She waited for him to be totally honest.

"I don't want to keep you from going, Amanda, but yes, I will miss you."

"Then come with me."

"Seriously?"

"Yes."

He smiled and kissed her sweetly, appearing as though he might start crying again, but he didn't.

"We have to trust Jesus to lead us on from here, Matthew."

He responded seriously. "And where are we, Amanda?"

"I don't know about you, but I'm completely in love."

"You're crazy."

"So are you."

"There's nothing crazy about a guy like me falling for a girl like you."

She smiled and asked him what he had gone to do. He had heard his parents coming upstairs and apologized to them privately about not going with them to the memorial service.

"You're a good son, Matthew," she said. "You might not do everything exactly the way they want you to, but I know you love them."

He sighed. "I do, but I hate to see them taking out their frustrations on you. They should be thanking God for you, not—" he couldn't say it, but she knew what he meant.

"Matthew, look at me."

He did and she smiled at him. "It doesn't matter to me what they think. You and me, we know the truth, and so does God. That's what matters."

"But it's not fair to you."

"And it's not fair to you they can't believe their son has changed. And I don't think anything we do or don't do is going to matter. God was the one who changed your heart. We'll have to wait for Him to do that in them too."

He kissed her again, and even though they were alone in his bedroom with the door closed, sitting on his bed, and his kisses were very tender and passionate, she allowed it. Whether his parents thought it was possible or not, their son had been transformed by the grace and love of God, and she trusted her Savior to continue His work in both of their hearts.

"I love you, Amanda," he said, kissing her forehead and holding her gently in his arms. "I can make it through this if you believe that."

"I believe it, Matthew. Love me all you want. I won't push an ounce of it away."

"And you'll love me back?"

"Yes, Matthew. I'll love you back. For as long as you let me."

He smiled and then laughed, falling back on the bed.

"What's so funny?"

"Oh, Amanda. I came up here to break up with you."

"What?"

"I can't let go," he said.

"Thank God for that," she laughed. "Should I be concerned this breakup could come any day?"

"No," he said softly, sitting up and taking her into his arms. "I want you for the rest of my life, Amanda."

Mandy resisted the urge to tease him and ask if that was an official proposal. She let the words enter her heart, knowing Matt wouldn't say such a thing flippantly. And she cherished the thought she could have this incredibly great guy for the rest of her life.

Chapter Nineteen

On Friday morning Colleen had to rush to make it to the counselor meeting on time. She had forgotten to set her alarm the night before, probably because she had been distracted by talking to Chris on the phone and feeling surprised by his disappointment she had met someone else and was no longer interested in having a relationship with him.

It surprised her because he had been the one who had decided to go to China for the summer and then made plans to be gone for an additional year while he spent time visiting his grandparents and living in Vietnam. He had been willing to leave, and she supposed she had translated his decision into the fact she wasn't as important to him as he was to her—a way she had often felt in their relationship. He was always busier than she was. He was always putting the priority on school, work, and ministries he was involved in—all noble things she didn't oppose, and yet they all seemed to be higher on his priority list than her.

And yet when she talked to him yesterday, he had sounded genuinely upset she didn't want to see him for another two weeks when she returned home from going to Shasta Lake with Blake's family, and that she had no intention of stopping her relationship with him.

On the phone she had been matter-of-fact about it. "I'm seeing someone else. He's going to be in California all year, but I want to continue seeing him anyway."

The more she had thought about it afterwards, the more she realized how it must have sounded to Chris. Whenever he'd had plans to leave, she hadn't wanted a long-distance relationship: a year and a half ago when he decided to go to Harvard instead of remaining local for college, and then this spring when he decided to travel overseas. And yet here she was, saying she had only been seeing Blake for a few weeks and he was leaving, and yet she wanted things to continue with him.

She hadn't slept well, and waking up late made her feel like a frazzled mess by the time she reached the meeting. Walking in quietly five minutes late, she saw Blake had already started making the announcements for the morning.

"You okay?" Amber whispered, welcoming her with a hug as she sat beside her.

"I overslept."

Blake was in the middle of telling them about a schedule change for the day, so she didn't expect him to acknowledge her in any way, and yet once he had finished with that announcement and allowed Tamara to say something, he didn't hesitate to catch her eye across the room and give her a look showing his concern and curiosity about why she had been late. She was never late.

She smiled at him, feeling it come naturally. Blake always made her smile. He winked at her, and the meeting took its usual course after that. She'd been having a good week with her campers, but she was glad it was Friday. She was looking forward to spending the day with Blake tomorrow. The time she'd had with him last Saturday made her smile also, and the conflicting thoughts of yesterday seemed to fade.

"You were late," he said after the meeting, sounding concerned. "Is everything all right?"

"I overslept," she said. "I must look a mess."

She ran her fingers through her dark hair above her forehead and held it away from her face. She'd had to brush the long strands quickly and knew they weren't as smooth and sleek as after she'd had a shower.

Blake leaned down and whispered in her ear. "Beautiful, Pocahontas. The word you're looking for is 'beautiful', not a mess."

She smiled and dropped her hand from her hair. Blake asked if she could meet him this afternoon like usual, and she said she would be there. She didn't know what it was about Blake Coleman, but every time she was feeling unsure about their relationship, he always made her feel she was meant to be with him. He never used those words or tried to persuade her, but he didn't have to use words. His presence was enough to touch her heart in a way no one else ever had.

"Are you and Adam going to Silver Falls tomorrow?" Kerri asked Lauren on the way up the hill to their cabins following the early morning counselor meeting.

"Yes," Lauren said, feeling her shy smile emerge.

"How are you feeling about it?"

She let out a nervous sigh. "Fine."

"Any reservations about it being just the two of you?"

Lauren knew why Kerri was asking her. She was always advising her friends, and girls she mentored, about being careful where they spent time alone with guys—both those they knew well and those they didn't.

Each week during the junior high and high school camps, Lauren had teamed up with Kerri to have a slumber party for their girls one night, either inside or outside, and Kerri would share about her bad experience when she was fourteen and then give the girls a chance to ask questions about dating and other teen girl issues they might be afraid to ask anyone else.

Lauren didn't take her friend's concerns lightly or see her as trying to put Adam into a category where he didn't belong. She knew Kerri was looking out for her, and she appreciated it.

"I'm not worried," she said. "Adam had plenty of chances to try something on Saturday. But I do hope we can talk about it—set some standards, you know? I think we both want the same thing, but I'm sure talking about it will help make it more than an ideal."

"Do you think you can bring it up if he doesn't?"

"Yes," she said. "I was really bold about saying things to him on Saturday. I always feel nervous when I know I'm going to be seeing him, but then when I'm actually with him I don't feel that way."

"I'll pray for you," Kerri said. "Something tells me Adam will want to talk about it too. I think Adam is the kind of guy you can expect the best from, not the worst. But if I'm wrong, then punch him!"

Lauren laughed. "With you being my best friend, and my brother being his senior counselor, I can't imagine him thinking he can get away with anything."

"You could make him ask Blake for permission to take you," Kerri said. "Dylan told me after he talked to my dad and asked for permission to start seeing me, it made him feel like he had to take good care of me, and Seth said the same thing when he and Amber were first dating. He asked her dad for permission, and it changed his view of her."

"Maybe I'll do that," Lauren said, liking the idea. She couldn't imagine Adam saying he wouldn't do that, and it would give her a more secure feeling if she knew her brother was aware of where they were going and would be asking Adam about it later.

Because tomorrow was Saturday, she decided not to take a chance on seeing Adam sometime today and waiting to talk to him about it then. She usually wrote him a note and left it in his mailbox sometime during the day. Going into her cabin to find all her girls awake and getting ready for the day, she took her pad of stationery from her shelf and went out on the porch to write him a note, including the request in a sweet but expectant way.

Mandy finished packing her bag, set it on the floor, and made the bed neatly. She was glad she had come to be with Matt this week, but she was ready to leave here and have time away from the grieving and watchful eyes of his parents. She liked them. She thought they were nice people. And she understood their concerns because Matt had often lied to them in the past and they really didn't know her, but it had been hard to be thought the worst of, especially during a difficult time when she would have liked to be a blessing to them instead of a burden, but she couldn't do anything about that, she supposed.

Taking her things downstairs, she set them by the door and went to find Matthew. He was in the living room, talking to his mom, and she entered the room quietly, sat beside him, and didn't try to interrupt in any way, but his mother stood shortly after her arrival and left the room to go make them lunch before they had to leave. Mandy tried not to let Mrs. Abramson's cool acknowledgment of her presence bother her, but after a week of being as strong as she knew how to be, the sting of it seemed too great to ignore.

"I'm sorry, baby," Matt said, seeing the pain in her eyes.

He pulled her close to him, and she let the tears fall quietly on his shoulder. She didn't want to make him feel bad, but she knew she couldn't hide her feelings from him either. He saw right through any masks she ever tried to wear with him. He always had.

"I'm all right," she said after a moment. Letting it out helped, and she reminded herself in another hour they would be on their way to Camp Laughing Water where many of their friends were. Tomorrow they would be heading for the beach. She expected it to be a good weekend.

"I can break up with you now if you want," he said, teasing her in his sweet way.

She smiled at him, remembering his words about wanting her for the rest of his life. Suddenly his mother's rude behavior seemed trivial. They loved each other, and they knew the truth. That's what mattered. His parents could love her, and she and Matthew could be hiding something. She would rather have it be this way.

After eating their lunch in the kitchen, they told his parents good-bye and left the house. Matt hadn't been able to give them a definite time of his return. He hadn't decided if he was going to remain at camp next week or come back here. Once they were on the freeway, heading out of Portland to their destination, Mandy began to wonder more seriously about what Matt would decide to do about school. They were supposed to be leaving two weeks from tomorrow along with Amber, Seth, and Kerri. On the one hand she could see Matt being more anxious than ever to go, but on the other she could understand him feeling like going away to college right now wasn't the best timing.

She decided to wait for him to mention it, and she prayed he would make the right decision and that it wouldn't be a huge burden to him. He'd had enough to face during this past week without adding a stressful decision about college on top of it. And she also decided that whatever he chose, she would support him. She hadn't realized it until this week, but Matthew's happiness was very important to her. She wanted him to be happy, and she wanted to do whatever she could to be a part of bringing him happiness.

***

Adam checked his mailbox at one-thirty and found a note from Lauren. The regular mail hadn't been delivered yet, but he had taken a quick swim to cool off on this hot August day, and he knew there would likely be one waiting for him. Taking the note and heading to his cabin where he would be meeting one of his guys who said he wanted to talk to him sometime today, Adam unfolded it and read Lauren's words. She wrote him every day, and he was always amazed. Amazed to get notes from a pretty girl he was crazy about, and amazed by her words.

Dear Adam,

Good morning! Well, it's morning for me right now. Good whenever for whenever you're reading this. I was just talking to Kerri about going with you to Silver Falls tomorrow, and I can't wait! I'm really glad you asked me, and I hope it can be a day where we get to know each other better and can relax after our long and busy week. You know, the kind of day where we can look back several months from now and say, "Remember when..." and the thought will bring a smile to our hearts.

I do have one request, and I hope you won't think this is too weird. I really do trust you, Adam, and I expect us to have a great time together, but I'm wondering if you would mind going to Blake and asking him for permission to take me there? It would mean a lot to me. And I think it would mean a lot to him too. He promised my parents he would take care of me this summer, and because of what happened with Kurt, I know he takes that seriously.

Anyway, I hope you have a great day, and I'll see you when I see you.

Love,
Angel

Chapter Twenty

Blake was in the staff office, finishing up his cabin assignments for next week when the door opened, and he turned to see someone step inside he didn't know. The young man had on a visitor's tag from the main office, so he knew he had already checked in with someone, but he appeared lost.

"Can I help you?" he asked.

"I'm looking for someone on staff this summer," he replied. He appeared to be college-age.

"Counseling or crew?" he asked, knowing if it was a crew person, he could check the assignment board and point him the right direction, but a counselor would be harder to find this time of day. During afternoon free time, counselors could be just about anywhere.

"Counseling," he said. "It's Colleen Garcia. Do you know where she might be?"

Blake took a moment to let that sink in. Colleen hadn't mentioned anyone coming to see her today. He could imagine the dark-haired guy being one of her brothers. She had two, and they were both older, but he'd never met them so he didn't know what they looked like. His features appeared to be more Asian than a mix of Hispanic and American Indian however. He asked anyway.

"Are you her brother?"

"No, a friend," he said.

"I'm not sure where she would be right now. I could have someone check her cabin, or she might be by the lake." Checking his watch and seeing it was an hour before he was scheduled to meet her, he dismissed their meeting spot as a possibility.

"I can wait," he said.

Blake took the radio from his hip, sending out a call for Tamara and waited for her to respond. He could usually reach her as long as she wasn't too far away, which he didn't expect her to be. She spent time with her counselors during the afternoons.

"I'm here," she said. "What's up?"

"Do you know where Colleen is? Someone is here to see her."

"I haven't seen her," she said. "Would you like me to check her cabin?"

"If you're close by," he said. "I'm at the office, so I could find someone else if you're busy."

"No, I'm right here," she said, stepping into the office at the same moment and speaking to him face-to-face. "I was on my way to see another counselor. I'll check and let you know."

Tamara saw the visitor standing there, and she stepped over to introduce herself. "Are you a friend of Colleen's?"

"Yes."

"Is she expecting you?"

"No. I thought I'd surprise her. Is that okay?"

"Yeah, that's fine. Can I give her your name?"

"Sure," he said. "It's Chris. Chris Logan."

"All right, Chris. I'm on my way there, and I'll let you know what I find out."

"Thank you," he said.

Blake felt like he was going to pass out. He'd never seen a picture of Chris, but it seemed obvious now he would be the most logical guy to be dropping in to see Colleen like this. She had talked to him on the phone yesterday. Colleen said she told him the truth and wasn't planning to see him until she was back home in a couple of weeks, but he knew it hadn't been an easy conversation for her to have. It hadn't gone as well as she had hoped.

"Excuse me," Blake said, trying to sound polite and acting as if he had somewhere else he needed to be. Tamara didn't have to ask why he followed her, and she didn't say anything until they were a considerable distance from the office.

"What do you think we should do?" she asked him. "Do you think it's a good idea for her to see him?"

"Can we stop her?"

"No, but I could tell her it would be better to wait until tomorrow. I can't have these kinds of things upsetting my counselors," she said, trying to sound playful about the situation.

"Did she talk to you about it?" he asked seriously.

"This morning," she said. "She seemed out of sorts at the meeting, and she told me she hadn't slept well. I heard the phone call yesterday went a little differently than she was expecting?"

"Yes."

"You okay?"

He sighed. "I don't know. I'm mostly concerned for Colleen. I don't know if her seeing him would be a good thing, but who am I to—" He couldn't finish.

"Someone who cares about her very much," Tamara said. "You wait here, and I'll go see if I can find her."

"I'll be in my room," he said. "If she wants to see me first, I'll let that be her choice."

***

Colleen gave her camper a hug and hoped her words had helped. She had known all week something was bothering Hannah, and the fifteen-year-old had been difficult to connect with emotionally, but she had managed to break through today and found out why Hannah had been so distant. One of her best friends had recently gone after an ex-boyfriend she had been hoping to get back together with, and she felt very hurt her friend would do that, and she also was having trouble coping with the reality that her boyfriend had suddenly stopped loving her for no apparent reason.

She didn't understand it all and wished it could be different, but she was beginning to see how God could help her to heal from the pain and move on. Colleen had encouraged her to believe God had someone else for her and to think carefully about who her friends really were and to get away from those who were being a negative influence on her or bringing her down with their hurtful behavior.

"Thanks for talking," Hannah said. "I feel better now."

"This is also an opportunity to see the reality of God in your life," she said, recalling how she'd had a time like that when she was fifteen. She told her about when her family had moved here from Arizona and she had been worried she wouldn't make any friends. "I prayed and asked God for a good friend, and I ended up meeting her on the first day of school and we've been best friends ever since. She's even the one who got me to come here this summer."

"Really?"

"Yep. If you ask God to show you He's real by providing new friends or something else you really need, I believe He will. He wants you to see Him, Hannah. Invite Him to show Himself to you in a tangible way like that, okay?"

"Okay," she said.

Colleen heard a knock on the closed cabin door, and she went to see who it was, supposing it might be a friend of one of her campers looking for someone, but it turned out to be Tamara.

"Am I interrupting anything?"

"No, I think we're about done. Give me a minute?"

"Sure," Tamara said.

Colleen closed the door and asked Hannah if she needed to talk more, or if she wanted to get going. She had said earlier she was meeting some friends at three, and it was already ten after.

"I should go," Hannah said. "One of those good friends I was telling you about is waiting for me."

Colleen waited for Hannah to put her shoes on and leave the cabin, and then she invited Tamara inside. No one else was here, and Tamara often checked on her and the other counselors during free time. She had talked to Tamara this morning about Chris and supposed her senior counselor was checking to see how she was doing and if she wanted to talk more. But Tamara had news for her instead.

"Chris is here," she said simply.

"Chris? He's here?"

"Do you want to see him?"

Colleen was shocked. This was not like Chris at all. He didn't drop in unannounced. In the year and a half they had dated, he'd never done anything spontaneous. His schedule was even more organized than hers and planned out days in advance. Yesterday she had told him she would see him when she returned home in another two weeks. She couldn't believe he would do this.

"I don't know," she said. "I mean, I guess I should since he came all this way. It's not that I don't want to, it's just—"

"Complicated?"

She nodded. "Really complicated."

"Do you want to talk to Blake first?"

"Do you know where he is?"

"Yes. And he knows Chris is here. He's the one who called me."

Colleen didn't have to think about her response. "Yes. I want to see him," she said, reaching for her sandals and slipping them on her bare feet. "Where is he?"

"In his room."

"And where is Chris?"

"At the office."

"Okay. Thanks. Pray for me."

"I will, honey."

Colleen took a back trail to Blake's room because if she went the normal way, it was possible Chris would spot her. She wasn't sure why she wanted to see Blake first, but she did, and she didn't feel the least bit guilty about it. One of the things Tamara had said to her this morning was Chris had been the one to leave, not her, so she didn't have anything to feel bad about if she had fallen in love with someone else. She realized that's how Chris had made her feel when she talked to him on the phone yesterday, like he couldn't believe she had gotten involved in another relationship so soon.

She didn't have to knock on Blake's door because he'd left it open, and he crossed the room as soon as he spotted her in the open doorway. She didn't hesitate to step into his arms and let him hold her. She didn't need Blake to tell her what to do, but she needed to be with him before she faced Chris.

She didn't expect to, but she started crying. She had tried to downplay how much talking to Chris yesterday had affected her, but now she realized how much his accusing words had hurt. She hadn't done anything wrong. She hadn't been looking for another relationship, it had just happened.

"I'm sorry, Colleen," Blake said, holding her gently. "If you want me to go away—" He couldn't finish his thought, and she didn't want him to think he was the problem. He had been nothing but patient and chivalrous through all of this. He had no way of knowing Chris would come back early any more than she did.

"Please don't," she said. "Don't let go of me, Blake. I need you to hang on to me right now."

"Okay," he laughed softly. "I will."

They were both silent for a moment, and Colleen felt something with Blake she knew without a doubt she had never felt with Chris. She felt like she belonged to him—like she was a special treasure he never wanted to let go.

"Do you want me to talk to him?" he asked seriously.

His words confirmed what she was thinking and made her smile. He was always so caring. So protective. So possessive of her, but in a good way. She liked it.

"No, I will," she said, feeling peace and courage enter her heart. She stepped back and looked into his sweet face. "I'm all right. I just needed to see you first."

He gave her a gentle smile, and if she hadn't already fallen in love with him, she did so now. He made everything easy and feel so right.

"Will you be here when I get back?" she asked.

"If you want me to be."

"I do," she said.

"I'll be here. Take whatever time you need."

She smiled. He had said that to her before, but in a different context. When he gave her the LOVE ring on her finger and told her he was serious about wanting something to happen with her that would last beyond this summer, he said he would be waiting whenever she decided she might want that too. He'd made his feelings for her clear but gave her the time she needed to decide if she wanted it.

She kissed him on the cheek and stepped away, heading for the office and feeling better than she had five minutes ago. Her inner strength wavered when she saw Chris waiting for her, but she asked Jesus for more and continued up the steps to the raised deck area.

Chris spotted her coming and rose from the bench. He seemed tentative about seeing her, and that gave her strength to initiate a hug. He was an important person in her life, and she had missed him. She hadn't been expecting to see him for at least another year, and seeing him much sooner brought a certain joy to her heart.

"Chris Logan! What on earth are you doing here?" She laughed and demanded an answer with her brown eyes staring up at him.

He smiled. "I'm not sure," he said. "I felt like I had to come see you. Are you mad?"

"No. I'm shocked. This isn't like you!"

"I know," he said. "I would have waited until tomorrow, but I thought I might miss you."

She didn't comment on that. She had told him yesterday she couldn't see him tomorrow like he was hoping because she had plans with Blake.

She knew they needed to go somewhere else to talk. There were too many campers hanging around here, but she wasn't certain where would be a good place. She asked Jesus to guide her in that too.

"Let's go for a walk," she said, turning back in the direction she had come, heading away from the main camp area. "How long can you stay?"

"As long as you want me to."

"I do have things to do later," she said. "But I have some spare time right now."

He didn't say anything for a minute, and neither did she. Once they were away from the main buildings, and the campers' voices were well in the distance, he stopped her with a gentle tug on her arm. She turned toward him and instantly found herself being kissed.

Gently she pushed herself away from him. She was neither shocked nor horrified by his display of affection, but she had no desire for it to continue. There had been a time she had loved kissing him, but she simply didn't feel the same way as she once had. She still cared about him and knew she would never forget him, but he didn't come close to touching her heart the way Blake did. Not now, not ever.

"I love you, Colleen," he said.

His words surprised her because he'd never said them before, but they also had almost no effect on her. She had waited a long time to hear him say those words, but it was too late.

"I know you don't understand, Chris, but I'm with someone else. I'm touched you came all this way, but—"

"Colleen. You've known this guy for two months. What about us? What about the last two years? Doesn't that mean anything to you?"

"Yes, it means tons to me, Chris. I care about you very much. I loved what we had together, but I wasn't in love with you. If I was, I wouldn't have gone out with another guy while you were away. I would have waited for you. But after you left, I didn't feel the need to do that. I wasn't looking for something else right away either, but when Blake came along, I let it happen."

"And you're in love with him?"

She couldn't hold back a smile. "Yes."

"After two months?"

"Actually, not that long," she said, refusing to let Chris' doubts become her own. "More like one month, but it's right. I feel it."

"And what we had? You never felt anything?"

"Yes, I did. But this is different."

"How is it different?"

She thought about that and told him the way she honestly felt. "We had friendship, and common interests, and I enjoyed our time together. But with Blake—I think I want to spend the rest of my life with him."

"It's not real, Colleen."

"What do you mean?"

"I mean, you can't know that after a month. You're in the 'everything's wonderful', feel-good stage. What about a month from now when he's away at school? How are you going to feel then? I was gone for a month, and you fell in love with somebody else."

His words stung. She didn't believe them, but they hurt. She started to say something, but she decided against it and turned away from him instead, breaking into a jog after a few steps and running all the way to the main camp area.

He didn't come after her, and once she arrived where they had started, she wasn't sure where to go. She wanted to talk to Blake, but maybe Chris was right. Maybe she was living a fairy-tale that was going to come crashing down in another two weeks when she went back to the real world and Blake decided he didn't really want her in his life.

He was older, more mature, more stable. She was flighty and directionless and thinking she could be in love after one great Saturday with him. She was acting like a child, not a mature young woman on the verge of the adult world.

Chapter Twenty-One

Blake saw Colleen running down the trail past his window and was out the door in a flash, catching up with her before she reached the fork heading into the girls' cabin area.

"Let me go," she said, sounding out-of breath and somewhat convincing but not enough for him.

He didn't say anything and gently pulled her against him. No one was around at the moment, but he knew that could change quickly.

"Come with me," he said, hoping she wouldn't resist, and she didn't, gently leaning into his side and allowing him to lead her toward his room.

When they arrived, he opened the door and led them both inside, closing the door behind them and not caring if it was against the rules to have a girl in his room. He knew his intentions were genuine and necessary.

She clung to him, and he simply held her. She didn't cry immediately, but eventually he heard some gentle sniffles.

"What happened?" he asked.

She didn't respond. He wondered if he should call Tamara on the radio and see if she could come, but he decided to wait. He wanted her to talk to him. He wanted to kiss her so badly, but he knew that would really be going against the rules, and he wasn't sure he could justify it, or if she would want that from him.

"Talk to me, Colleen," he said. "If you don't talk, I'm going to have to kick you out of here."

"He wants me back," she said, stepping away from him. "He says he loves me."

Blake would have felt alarmed except Colleen didn't sound excited about either of those. He asked to be sure. "How do you feel about that?"

"I don't want him back. I love you."

"Did you tell him that?"

"Yes."

"What did he say?"

"That it's new and exciting and I'm mistaking that for love; what I feel for you can't possibly be real."

"Do you believe that?"

She didn't respond.

Blake searched his heart. He had wondered if this was real or something fooling his heart into thinking it was significant. They were in a unique environment. Someplace they saw each other every day and were unaffected by the real world. What would happen in another week when they left this place? What would happen when they were apart for weeks at a time? What would happen when *he* was hundreds of miles away and Chris was right there on the same college campus with Colleen?

He pulled her close to him again and said the only thing he knew for sure. "I love you, Colleen. I don't know what the future will bring, but I know I love you."

She didn't say anything, and he held her, feeling like he never wanted to let go. But he knew he had to. They couldn't stay in here all day.

"Do you want me to call Tamara?" he asked. "Have her meet you somewhere?"

She stepped back and dried her cheeks with her fingertips. "Yes," she nodded. "Thank you."

He reached for his radio and called Tamara. She was right across the deck in her room, and he said he would be there in a minute. He didn't share any details because they weren't the only ones listening on this frequency.

Colleen gave him a hug before she stepped away. "I'm sorry," she whispered.

"Don't be," he said. "I want you to be happy, Colleen. Whatever that means."

She stepped back and smiled at him. "I'm happy when I'm with you. Always."

"Even now?"

"Yes."

She stepped away and went out. He stood there, staring at the closed door, then sat on his bed and did what he had been doing while Colleen was talking to Chris. He prayed. He asked God to direct their steps, whether they were on the same paths or different ones. He wanted what was best, and he trusted Jesus to know that better than he did.

* * *

Adam knocked on Blake's door, and Blake opened it immediately, but he appeared to have been expecting someone else.

205

"Oh, hey, Adam."

He smiled. "Expecting someone else?"

He laughed. "Yeah, but it's probably good it's you. What can I do for you today?"

"I came to ask your permission for something," he said, trying to sound businesslike, as if this had something to do with Blake being his senior counselor instead of his girlfriend's older brother.

"Shoot," he said. "At this point in the summer, I'm ready to say yes to just about anything."

Adam smiled and stepped inside the room. "Actually this is a personal matter, so you might not want to say that too quickly."

"Oh? And would this personal matter be my sister?"

"That's the one."

"Okay, let me have it, Buzz," he said, crossing his arms in front of his chest.

Adam didn't feel worried about asking Blake for permission to take Lauren to Silver Falls tomorrow, but he wanted to let Blake know he took it seriously, and so he asked seriously.

"I'd like to take Lauren to Silver Falls for the day tomorrow, if that's all right with you."

"Silver Falls? Just the two of you?" Blake clarified.

"Yep."

Blake smiled. "And what exactly are your intentions?"

"Just to have a nice day with her. Last Saturday was the first time I've spent any time alone with her, and I think we need that. Lauren needs to know I'm serious about this. I don't see her as just another girl.

I see her as someone I could have a serious, long-lasting relationship with."

Blake gave him an interesting look and asked him something he got the feeling didn't have to do with him and Lauren. "How do you know that?"

"How do I know she's different?"

"Yeah."

"I don't know, man. I just do. Last Saturday was like—" he searched for the right word.

"Moments in paradise?" Blake said.

"Yes, exactly."

Blake seemed to be somewhere else.

"You all right?" Adam asked.

"Yes," he said, breaking out of it. "And yes, you can take my sister wherever she is willing to go with you. Just take care of her."

"I will, boss. And I'm glad you're going to be at college with us. Keep me in line, all right?"

"I will, Adam," he said, reaching out to shake his hand and then pulling him into a hug as well. "Just be honest with my sister, and let her know exactly how you feel. If she's happy, I'll be happy."

Another light knock tapped on the semi-open door, and Blake looked past Adam to see Matt peek inside. He had been expecting him anytime, and it was good to see him.

"Hey, Matt," he said, stepping over to welcome him. He had wanted to go to the memorial service, but he hadn't been able to get away. "Good to see you."

"Good to be here," Matt replied. "Hey, Adam."

Adam welcomed him similarly, and Blake noticed Matt's girlfriend was with him. He had met Mandy a couple of times this summer, and he said hello to her as he saw Colleen coming out of Tamara's room across the open deck of the housing area.

She spotted him and smiled. He wanted to go to her, but he had his hands full here. Breaking away from the group anyway, he wanted to make sure she was okay. She looked better than she had twenty minutes ago, and he told her so.

"I feel better now," she said. "Would it be all right if we didn't meet today? I have a couple of things I need to do before dinner, and it looks like you're busy anyway."

"Yeah," he said, wondering what she needed to do, but he didn't ask. "But if you need to talk, I can make the time."

"I'm all right. Thanks for coming after me. I'd be a mess otherwise, but Tamara said things that made me feel better. I'll tell you about it later. I want to say hi to my friends over there."

He could tell she felt better, and they walked to the huddled group. Mandy stepped over to meet Colleen. They knew each other from back home and held each other for a long time. Colleen hugged Matt also and expressed her sympathy for his loss.

"I'm on my way to see Amber," she told Mandy. "Do you want to come with me?

"Sure," she said, turning to Matt and asking where he would be later.

"I'll come find you," he said. "I'll find out where we're sleeping and let you know."

"Okay," she said, giving him a sweet expression before stepping away, and Blake could see one reason why Matt seemed to be doing so well. After Adam stepped away, Blake invited Matt into his room to talk more privately, and he stated the obvious.

"Looks like you've fallen into a little bit of love there, Spider-Man."

"You have no idea," he said. "Or maybe you do. I heard things are progressing between you and Pocahontas."

He didn't deny it, but he did wonder where he and Colleen stood. Would she want to go to the beach with him tomorrow like they'd planned? Was everything the same as it had been all week, or had Chris' letter and visit changed that?

"I'm beginning to wonder if a change in my school plans might be in order," Blake said. "I'm having a difficult time imagining heading back to California in two weeks."

"That serious, huh?"

"That serious," he said. "How do they do that?"

Matt laughed. "I have no idea, and I'm facing the same problem."

"What's that?"

"I'm thinking about not going to school, and I know having Amanda go without me will make my heart snap in two."

"Ah," he said. "Have you talked to her about it?"

"Not yet. I'm planning to sometime this weekend, but I'm not looking forward to it."

Blake was planning to do the same with Colleen. He wanted to know how she felt so he could think about it more seriously. After what Adam had said about being glad he was going to be with them at Lifegate, he could see how God might want him to stick with his original plans, but with what had happened between Colleen and Chris, he could equally justify needing to remain here in Oregon for his senior year.

"Are you still up for tonight?" Blake asked Matt, getting to the immediate matter at hand.

"Yep. Just tell me when, and I'm there."

"Did you know I had a little brother who was killed a few years ago?"

"No. When?"

Blake told him the story about Kurt, and he was reminded the pain of it all could come back in a hurry. He had always regretted not being there that weekend. He possibly could have prevented it and had no chance to say good-bye.

"I don't think it's fully sunk in yet," Matt admitted. "I feel like he's on a trip with some friends or something."

"Is that why you want to stay instead of going to school right now?"

"Maybe. But it's more for my parents than me. I haven't been home all summer, and now Mark's gone. Going away seems heartless, I guess. Especially since I've caused them grief in the past."

"Seth said you've had some trouble over that this week."

"Yes. I didn't realize it until now, but they don't think I've really changed. They don't think Amanda is good for me, although they couldn't be more wrong about that. I hate to think where I would be right now if she hadn't been there."

"How long are you planning to stay here?"

"We're going on her staff trip tomorrow, and then I don't know. We might come back here, or I might take her home so she can have time with her family. I'm just taking it one day at a time."

Blake supposed he was going to have to do the same. Right now he didn't know if he would be spending the day with Colleen tomorrow, let alone this fall or for the rest of his life.

He ended up not seeing her until after campfire time when Matt gave a very moving and honest testimony of his own past, his brother's recent choices, and how he was going to go on from this tragedy. His words about living each day celebrating the life he could have if he followed Jesus and loved God with all of his heart spoke the most to Blake, and he knew he needed to do the same.

During the late-night beach party that followed where the campers could enjoy good food, music, and hanging out with their friends at the end of the week, Blake made a point to talk to Colleen when he spotted her alone at the food table while the campers were heavily distracted by the finals of the limbo contest. He wanted to let her know he had been thinking of her, and he also wanted to ask her something before it was time for bed. He didn't usually have a chance to talk to her on Saturday morning until all the campers had left and it was time for them to be dismissed from their duties for the day.

He didn't try to disguise his approach. No one was watching, and he stepped in front of where she was walking down the line grabbing various food items. She looked up at him and smiled.

"Hey, you're in my way. I want those last Oreos."

He stepped over, and she reached past him to grab the remaining ones on the plate.

"Is all of that for you?"

"Absolutely," she said. "I don't share Oreos with anybody."

"You're in a good mood," he commented.

She smiled at him in a way that always made him feel like he was going to pass out. "Of course I am," she whispered. "I'm going to the beach with my boyfriend tomorrow."

"Are you?"

"I hope so," she laughed. "You have something you need to tell me?"

"No."

She pulled something from her back pocket and handed it to him. It was an envelope folded in half. "Sorry it got a little wrinkled, but I wanted to give you this before you went to bed tonight."

"What is it?"

She turned away, gave him that smile again, and said over her shoulder, "You'll see. Sweet dreams."

Chapter Twenty-Two

Blake pulled the envelope from his pocket and sat down on the steps near his room to read Colleen's words. He'd had to wait until now to look at the note she had given to him at the party. There hadn't been enough light there to see it, and he'd had things to do with wrapping up the party and helping clean up. He had just finished making his cabin rounds and was ready to head for bed, but since Matt was sleeping in the spare bunk in his room tonight, he wanted to read her note before he went inside.

Dear Blake,

I'm sorry today was a little crazy. It seems like all summer I've been looking for an excuse to not be with you, but nothing could keep me from spending time with you for long, and now that I know I want this and have allowed it to happen, the biggest excuse of all showed up today, and it did shake me up, but not enough to push you away. Not now. Not after last Saturday. Not after a week where I have felt so much joy and peace about being your girlfriend. Not after talking to Tamara and hearing her say things about the guy she's been dating for two and a half years that match the way I feel about you. I love you, Blake, and I know it's real. And I hope it lasts for a long time.

Today when I was talking to Tamara, I remembered a poem Amber had read to me once that she had written for Seth. I remembered it because at the time I knew I didn't feel that way about Chris, and so I didn't care for it. But God brought it to my mind this afternoon, and I couldn't remember the exact words, but when I asked Amber if she had a copy of it, and she read it to me, I knew instantly the words she wrote for Seth are the way I feel about you. Don't worry about me going back to Chris and leaving your heart hanging out to dry, because it's not going to happen. I love you, and I can't wait until tomorrow.

When I see you
I don't just see you
but who you are with me

When I see you
I don't just see you now
but where we can go from here

When I see you
I see what has happened
since my love has entered your heart

When I see you
I see who I can be
If I believe in your love for me

When I see you
I see you as we are meant to be
—together

> *Always, my love,*
> *Colleen*

***

"What would you like to do today?" Seth asked Amber on Saturday morning after they had told Matt and Mandy good-bye. He thought it was a good idea for Matt to go on Mandy's staff beach trip with her, but it left them on their own today, something they hadn't encountered much this summer. They'd usually either spent their Saturdays with a group, with Matt and Mandy, or with Amber's brother, Ben, and his fiancée, Hope. They were a possibility today, but he hadn't talked to Ben yet.

Amber smiled at him in a dangerous way and said, "I don't know, sweet thing. What do you want to do?"

It had been an emotional week, and he knew he would love to have Amber all to himself today. Last year at this time they had gone to the beach together, just the two of them, and since this weekend marked the two-year anniversary of their first canoe-ride date, he could imagine that kind of day being a nice option, but he didn't know how wise it would be. Sometimes he felt strong and in control of his desires, and other times he felt weak. He felt that way today, and he knew it.

He smiled and whispered his answer in her ear. "I want to go to a beachside inn and stay there with you all day."

"Uh-oh," she laughed. "One of those days, huh?"

He nodded and pulled her close to him, giving her a loving hug and wishing she was more than his fiancée.

"It sounds like maybe we should see what Ben and Hope are doing today," she suggested.

"That would probably be good."

"I'll go find them. Are you going to wait here, or do you have something you need to do before we leave?"

"I'll wait here," he said, seeing Kerri saying good-bye to Lauren and Adam. He said a quick prayer for them and hoped they had a nice day today.

Adam had talked to him yesterday about the standards he and Amber had set for themselves early in their relationship, and he knew Adam planned on talking to Lauren about that today. Seth knew he needed to follow his own advice about avoiding being alone with his girlfriend when he was feeling weak. That was often when he wanted to the most, but he didn't allow himself to justify it—ever. Amber meant too much to him to hurt her in that way, and their relationship was more important to him than selfish moments of fleeting pleasure.

Kerri wandered his direction after Lauren and Adam left together, and Seth asked what her plans were.

"I don't know," she said. "I wonder what Chad and Jess are doing?"

"We should all go to the beach," he said, remembering that had been his original plan for this weekend. Not knowing what Matt would end up doing today, he had wanted to keep his schedule clear, but since he was with Mandy, they didn't have any reason to stick around here.

"That would be fun," she said. "I'm up for whatever. I need to clean my cabin first though. My girls were messy this week. Don't leave without me."

"Okay," he said, wondering if Blake and Colleen had left yet. He knew they were planning to go to the beach today too, and he knew the more people he could surround himself with, the better.

When Amber returned, she said Ben and Hope had no plans and would be happy to do something with them. Seth shared his idea of a bunch of them going to the beach, and they decided to try and find as many as they could to see who wanted to go. By noon they were on their way, and Seth felt much better about leaving the camp grounds with Amber in the seat beside him, Chad, Jessica, and Kerri in the back, and another two cars following them.

Seth had always been proud of his sister, but she had matured a lot over the course of this summer. He had watched her take a first serious stab at dating, make some wise but risky decisions about giving herself the freedom to fall in love, and even though she could have any unattached guy here this summer, she had remained true to her high standards and focused more on her relationship with God and the ministry than the guys constantly trying to get her attention. And here she was today, going along with a group made up of five other couples, and she was the only one without a date, and yet she seemed perfectly happy.

He couldn't help but wonder whom she might meet at Lifegate this year. Now that she'd had her first dating experience, and she was going to a school where there would be plenty of quality guys to choose from, he could picture her giving more of them a chance than she had thus far. Not that he thought she should or was especially looking forward to it, but he could see her being more ready to find her one true love. He would have to be someone unique, like Dylan. Someone who was truly one-of-a-kind, just like she was.

***

Lauren felt nervous on the drive to Silver Falls with Adam. He seemed his usual self, and she felt happy he had talked to Blake about their plans for today. But last weekend had been spontaneous, and everything had just sort of happened. This time she'd had all week to think and had placed expectations on herself about how she should act today. She didn't feel as confident as she had in her mind.

They talked about their respective weeks, and she had exciting things to share with him about decisions her girls had made. Last week she'd had a difficult time and felt like none of the girls in her cabin cared about anything she had to say. She felt inferior to them. Age-wise they were younger, mostly fifteen and sixteen, but in terms of their experiences, they had all been "out-there" more than she had with dating and being knowledgeable about the latest trends, fashions, and issues.

They had laughed when she mentioned the idea of holding off on dating or only dating guys who knew God or were at least interested in that. She hadn't dared to be honest about her own inexperience. Normally she was straightforward about it, but those girls had made her feel naive and stupid.

Her girls this week had been much more pleasant. They had been the same ages as the girls from the previous week, and several of them were very pretty and outgoing, but they also seemed more willing to hear about her advice on friendship and dating. And they asked good questions about God and spiritual matters she felt she had answered accurately and in a way they could apply to their lives.

Several of them had opened up to her when she talked to them individually too, and she was able to share about God's forgiveness for mistakes they had made, His unconditional and deep love for them, and how to truly seek a relationship with Jesus.

"I told them about you last night," she said. Adam had been listening to her talk for ten minutes straight, and she hoped he wasn't faking his interest, but this was the stuff that mattered to her.

"Oh, yeah?" he said, reaching over and taking her hand. "What did you say?"

"I told them you're the first guy I've ever kissed and how glad I am I waited for the right time."

"Did you tell them how much you let me kiss you?"

"No, I didn't give them details," she laughed. "I just said you are a very nice and decent guy who loves Jesus, and that after spending the day with you, I knew you were someone I felt comfortable letting into my space, and so when you asked if you could kiss me, I said yes. And they all were like, 'He asked permission? Oh, that's so sweet. Guys never ask me permission, they just do it.'"

Adam smiled. "I'm going to be asking you in another twenty minutes. Are you going to tell me yes today, Angel?"

"That's my plan," she said, feeling a comfortable closeness with him once again.

"I have something I want to talk to you about today," he said. "Something I talked to Seth about yesterday. Don't let me back out of it, okay?"

She gave a mock gasp. "Did you blab my secret?"

He laughed. "Yes, I told Seth the only guy you wanted more than me was him, and he said, 'Ah, I'm tired of Amber anyway, let's switch.'"

She laughed but then corrected what he said. "I never said I liked Seth more than you, I just told you about him first because I was too shy to admit the whole truth."

"And when did that change? When did you feel you could be totally honest with me?"

"When I knew you wanted to spend time with me instead of it only ending up that way."

"Did Blake tell you what I said when I asked him for permission to spend today alone with you?"

"No."

"I told him I wanted to do this to let you know how serious I am about us dating. This isn't an average day for me, Angel. This is something that could decide the course of my life."

"Oh, is that all?" she smiled. "I thought this was your way of getting your fill of Oregon beauty before leaving for California."

He lifted her hand to his lips and kissed her fingers softly. "I'm taking this Oregon Beauty with me to California," he said. "And who knows? In another few years I could find myself married to an angel."

Lauren thought of a verse she had shared with her campers this summer. God had brought it to her attention during training week, and all summer she had seen the truth of it in various ways, but none more so than in this. She had been praying for the right guy, and she had felt content to wait for God to bring him along at just the right time. And He had.

Taste and see that the LORD is good. Oh, the joys of those who trust in him!

Chapter Twenty-Three

From the moment Matt arrived at Camp Cold Springs with Mandy, he felt accepted and welcome by her friends. Everyone there obviously loved her, and their concern for her was naturally transferred to him as he finished out this difficult week by her side. He had expected to feel like an intruder with this small, tight-knit group as they spent this final weekend together as a staff, but he didn't for even a moment.

Mandy needed to get a few things from her cabin. Someone else had been sleeping there all week but had left everything the way she usually kept it. Other than her sleeping bag being rolled up and put on the top shelf of her small closet, everything else was in its place, and she was able to pack quickly for their overnight trip.

Guys weren't normally allowed in girls' cabins and vice-versa, but Matt was able to go with her because it was the end of the summer and no one was here besides the staff. Most of them were ready to go, and the vans and cars were leaving in ten minutes, so they didn't have much time, but that didn't stop him from giving her several sweet kisses before they went out the door. He had gotten used to kissing her every day, and the last twenty-four hours when he couldn't do that had just about killed him. He had no idea how he had survived being away from her for days at a time this summer, and he had no idea how he could ever go back to that.

Yesterday he had left his parents' house planning to talk to her about not going to school this fall, but now he didn't know if he could do it. They'd already spent enough time apart. He needed her every day, and he didn't want her to think otherwise.

One thing he had noticed about Amanda was she needed constant affirmation he wanted to be with her. He had been shocked several times when he left her on Saturday evening with sweet kisses and words that let her know exactly how he felt about her and then would see her a week later and she would be doubting his feelings for her again. He didn't want her living like that for weeks. He wanted her to know how special she was to him, but he knew saying, 'I'm not going with you to California' wouldn't say that very well.

"Have you forgotten yet?" he asked, moving his kisses from her lips to her cheek and close to her ear.

"Forgotten what?"

"That I love you."

She giggled. "No."

"Don't forget, okay?" he whispered in her ear.

"Okay," she said.

He returned his lips to hers and kissed her passionately. Visions of kissing her like this before sending her off to bed in her dorm room flashed through his mind, and for the moment any thoughts of being anywhere besides as close to her as possible seemed impossible. He had to go. He had to be with her. She needed him and he needed her. This was supposed to be their time. Away from his family and their accusing eyes. With their friends in a good, safe environment together. God had led them to the same school even before they knew each other. It was meant to be, wasn't it?

"We'd better go," she said, and he knew she was right. Before they stepped out of the cabin, he told her one more thing.

"I want you to have time with your friends, Amanda. Don't feel like you have to hang around with me all the time, okay? As long as I can be near you and see you, I'll be fine."

"I didn't ask you to come so I could ignore you, Matthew. I want time with you *with* my other friends, not time with my friends at the expense of not being with you."

He almost said, 'We'll have plenty of time together after this weekend,' but he didn't know that for sure, so he didn't respond. He wondered if she already knew what he was thinking. She hadn't said anything about it, but neither had he.

They rode with her friends Jenn and Jeremiah in Jenn's car, and Matt enjoyed the hour-long drive to the beach campsite. Amanda sat beside him in the middle of the back seat, and he held her in his arms the whole way. When they arrived at their destination, they helped with setting up the tents in two campsites adjacent to each other. One for the guys and one for the girls. Jeremiah told him he could be in his tent along with one other guy, and Matt put his stuff in there and then the whole group basically had free time until four o'clock when Isaac wanted them all to gather back here to talk about the summer.

Everyone walked to the beach to enjoy the sunny day, and Matt tried to lay low and not be the center of attention like he often was in a group setting, and that was easier to do when he didn't know the others well, but he found himself answering a lot of questions about his brother and the week. He didn't mind, but it was a constant reminder his life was never going to be the same. Everything had changed in a matter of days, and with as optimistic as he had often felt this week and how confidently he had talked to the high school kids last night about embracing life with God, as the afternoon wore on he had a more difficult time looking at it like that.

He didn't want to think about being away from Amanda, and yet it was there, like a dull pain that wouldn't go away. He tried to ignore it, to push it away, but it remained just the same.

***

Kerri didn't mind being the only one in their group without a date today, but she did feel concerned she might be a third-wheel anytime she found herself alone with one of the couples along for the day-trip to the romantic location. She hung around with Chad and Jessica the most, who weren't in the "We want to be alone" stage yet. They seemed to be having fun together and getting to know each other, and if anything, Kerri knew she could add to that instead of take away from it. She knew both Chad and Jess better than they knew each other, and she often had a story to share about one that the other enjoyed hearing.

After spending some time shopping and viewing the many attractions along the Newport Pier, the group decided to go to the beach, and Kerri was fine with sitting on a blanket and talking with whomever chose to sit beside her at any given time. First it was Chad and Jess and then when they went for a walk, Amber and Seth came to sit with her while they took a break from their kite-flying attempts. It was almost not windy enough today, which was really unusual for the Oregon Coast.

"Do you two have any idea when you're getting married?" she asked them.

"Not really," Seth said. "We're thinking of waiting until we know what we're doing next summer and then figuring out when would be the best time. We're getting married in Amber's backyard, so we don't have to worry about getting a date set far enough in advance to reserve the church or something."

"You're getting married in her backyard? When did you decide that?"

"When we went to Eric and Lora's wedding," Amber replied.

"Wasn't that before you were engaged?"

"Yes," Seth said, smiling sweetly at his fiancée. "But we were talking about it."

"And how long did you talk about it? Even before the summer?"

"Yes," Seth said. "A few weeks before school ended. When Ben and Hope got engaged."

Kerri thought of all the couples she had come with today and realized most of them could be married before she found a boyfriend she liked seriously. Ben and Hope were getting married in December. Amber and Seth next summer along with Kenny and Stacey. Blake and Colleen had just started dating, but Blake was a senior this year, so she could imagine them not waiting too long if things continued at this pace between them. The only ones she could see waiting longer were Chad and Jessica. She could see them remaining together on a long-term basis, but she also could see them taking a slower pace than a couple like Colleen and Blake.

She wondered how Lauren and Adam were doing today, and she said a prayer for them. Lauren had said she felt like she needed to know exactly what Adam was thinking before they went to Lifegate in two weeks. And Kerri could understand why she felt that way after what she had experienced with Dylan. She had always tried to be really honest with him about what she was thinking and feeling, and she felt he had done the same with her, and that had made their relationship fun and enjoyable for the most part, even in the end when she let him go.

Kerri asked Amber if she knew exactly what happened between Chris and Colleen this week. She'd heard bits and pieces and knew he had been at camp yesterday, but she hadn't seen him or heard the complete story. Amber told her what she knew, which she had mostly heard form Colleen herself, although Seth had talked to Chris also, and Kerri could relate to what Colleen felt about not missing Chris and how that had helped her to see he wasn't the guy she was meant to be with forever. She felt that way about Dylan too. Any time they'd had together was always nice, and she had looked forward to seeing him last weekend, but she hadn't missed him like she knew Amber would miss Seth if she was away from him for two months.

She wondered what exactly would make her feel differently about someone. Was it a matter of finding the exact person God had for her, or could she feel that way about more than one person and it would be whomever she met first? Knowing what she knew about the couples around her, she knew it could be someone she met in two weeks, and two months from now she could be completely in love with him. Or it could be someone she had already met or would meet at some point in the future, but it would take her a long time to feel that way.

Right now she was both looking forward to and dreading the prospect of meeting that person and falling in love. She had never imagined it being so unpredictable, open-ended, and complicated.

***

Blake had seen Colleen express many different emotions this summer. She had been cautious and reserved. She had been spontaneous. She'd been confused and insightful. She had been upset yesterday afternoon but then the happiest he had ever seen her last night. And today she definitely seemed happy, but also calm and content. After he had accepted Seth's invitation to go to the beach with the others, he had worried Colleen would be disappointed they couldn't have this day to themselves, but she hadn't expressed any such feelings, verbally or non-verbally.

"Is it okay we're sharing this day with everyone?" he asked once they were completely alone on the sunny ocean shore.

"Yeah, it's fine," she said. "I'm probably not going to be seeing most of them much after next weekend."

He knew the perfect opportunity had come to share his heart with her. He had no idea what this conversation would result in, but he wanted to know how she felt about their impending separation.

"You know I would move to Portland for you, if that's what you want me to do."

"You would?" she asked, sounding surprised.

"Yes. Is that what you want?"

"Is that what you want?" she fired back.

"I asked you first."

"No, Blake. This is not the kind of thing I should be deciding for us. You're a senior. I'm only a freshman with no idea what I want to do with my future. This is your call, not mine."

"But I want to know what you want."

"Of course I want you in Portland. I won't deny that. But I also want what is best, and I don't think I can know that about this. Only you can know what is best for you right now, Blake, and yes, I will miss you, but I'll be okay. I would rather have you be where you think you should be, than for us to be together and have you be unhappy."

He didn't say anything for a minute. He thought seriously about how his heart was leading him, and he honestly didn't feel that God wanted him in Portland right now. He loved Lifegate. It had become his home over the last three years. He had his work there and his ministries, both on campus and off. There were some classes he was looking forward to taking this year, and he knew all the teachers well by now. And then there was his sister being there, which he was excited about, and he knew if there was any time she needed him to be around as her big brother, this year would be that time.

He shared all of that with Colleen, and he knew it would be easier for her to transfer to Lifegate next semester or someplace close to where he got a job next year than for him to change his plans at this point. But he was willing to take the more complicated road if she needed that.

"I don't, Blake. I'm actually glad we're going to be apart because I think it will show me if what I feel for you is temporary or something that is going to last. Chris and I didn't survive being separated, and if he hadn't left this summer, I think we would still be together, but only because that would be the easy and comfortable thing to do."

"What do you need from me, Colleen? How can I be a real part of your life even when we're apart?"

"I need you to make me a part of your life. You did that this summer. I'm not exactly sure how, but you did. I know I matter to you, and I'm not sure I ever felt that with Chris. We liked each other. We had fun together. But I never felt like he needed me."

"I do need you," he said. "Yesterday when I thought I might be losing you, I couldn't breathe. I just met you this summer and I was doing fine before, but going on without you would be unbearable."

She put her arms around his neck and gave him a sweet smile. "Then I'll try to not let that happen. I can love you from a distance as long as I know you're doing the same."

"I will be," he said, kissing her tenderly and lingering like he wanted to. It was the first time he had kissed her seriously today, and he was reminded of their time together at Crater Lake and how amazing she made him feel. It was the same now, only he felt more certain this is what she wanted.

"I have something for you," he said, taking a small box from his pocket and handing it to her. He had seen something at one of the little shops they'd been in earlier.

She opened the clamshell case and smiled at the earrings he had selected. They were simple gold hearts, and that's the way he saw her. Someone who was easy to love and was simply beautiful. He felt amazed his persistent but simple efforts to woo her had actually paid off. He didn't have anything to offer her except himself.

"Thank you," she said, taking out the earrings she was currently wearing and replacing them with the hearts.

"I love you, Colleen," he said, slipping his arms around her waist and holding her close to him. "And I love that you're mine."

"Am I?" she asked.

He looked into her eyes. One of the things he had asked himself was why he felt the need to pursue this girl who was three years younger than him, barely out of high school, and not set on one particular path for her life. She was smart and mature for her age, but he remembered being eighteen, and he knew there was a world of difference between where he had been and where he was now.

Next year he would be working a real job as a youth pastor, and she could be trying to decide what to major in. She might be ready to marry him by next summer, or she might not be ready for several more years. She had plans to go to school in Portland, and he was going back to California. She was coming off a relationship and had freely admitted she didn't feel ready for another one. He'd been doing fine without a girl in his life, but despite all of that, he couldn't help himself. He had to pursue her. He had to tell her how she made him feel. He had to be around her as much as she would allow him to be.

"You know what I see when I see you?" he asked.

"What?"

"I see someone I was meant to love. I can't explain how I know that, but I do."

She smiled. "I can't explain it either, but I feel the same way, Blake. I tried not to, but I ended up here anyway."

Chapter Twenty-Four

Adam held Lauren's hand as they walked on the wide path carved into the rock behind the cascading waterfall. He laughed when she admitted her fear of heights and used it as an excuse to pull her closer to him as they walked along the trail with the thunderous sound of water coming off the hillside above them and tumbling into the creek bed a hundred feet below.

Once they were beyond the exposed hillside and onto more secure terrain, he didn't let go of her waist, and they walked to where they could view the waterfall from a more safe location, stopping to enjoy the beautiful sight. Adam had been here several times before, and Lauren had been here once, but neither of them had ever been here on a date, and Adam could already see how different this day would be from any other time.

When he had mentioned to Amber he was bringing Lauren here today, her eyes had lit up and she said, 'You'd better watch out, Adam. You'll never be able to think of that place the same way again.'

He could already see what she meant. He'd always seen this as a beautiful place, but with Lauren at his side, it became magical—like a piece of Paradise right here on Earth. With the rushing waterfall, gentle flowing creek, lush green foliage, and the blue skies overhead, he could imagine the Garden of Eden had been something like this.

There were too many people in this well-visited area for him to feel comfortable kissing her, but he knew there would be plenty more private spots further down the trail. He took her hand, and they walked with the wide creek flowing alongside them, playing peek-a-boo as it disappeared behind thick groves of trees and a gentle-sloping hillside. Adam kept a careful watch on the water, looking for something in particular, and after fifteen minutes of walking, he saw it.

The last time he had been here, he'd seen a guy and girl sitting in the middle of the creek in a shallow area where there were exposed, flat rocks sitting above the water's surface. They had been sitting there close to each other in the afternoon sun, and he had a vision of himself and Kerri sitting there like that.

He wasn't thinking about Kerri today. He had no desire to be with anyone besides Lauren now, but he wanted to take her out there and sit with her like that for a couple of reasons. He thought it would be romantic, like when they had sat and talked by the river last Saturday, and he also knew it would be a good location where they could talk about private things without being overheard, he could kiss her, and he wouldn't go further physically with Lauren than he should. Anyone walking by would plainly see them sitting out there together. It was private but not too private.

"Do you mind getting your feet wet?" he asked, beginning to remove his shoes. "I can carry you, but I might make us both fall."

She laughed and sat down to remove her tennis shoes also. "I think I'll walk," she said. "I don't mind getting my feet wet, but my clothes are another story."

They left their shoes on the edge of the shore and waded out to one of the large, flat rocks. It had moss growing along the cracks but otherwise was smooth and clean. They sat beside each other in a sunny spot. Adam looked around at their surroundings, and he really did feel like he was in the middle of Paradise and like they were the only two people here. The trail was visible, but anyone walking by took a major back seat to the beauty of the hillsides and gentle water flowing around them, not to mention Lauren herself.

"What's that smile for, Angel?"

"For the way I feel."

"And how do you feel?"

She leaned back on her hands and dangled her feet in the cool water. "Like this is a dream I never want to wake up from."

He leaned over and kissed her easily. Once, and then several more times.

"I don't want to wake up either," he said.

***

Mandy knew something was bothering Matt, and she kept waiting for him to say something to explain his subdued mood, but he didn't. It could just be a hard day, she supposed. He'd had moments this week where he would be fine, and then suddenly reality would hit him, and he would become more quiet and reflective.

When it was time to head back to the campsite for the staff gathering, he told her to go ahead without him. He wanted to be alone for awhile, he said, and she respected that. He hadn't had any time alone since Thursday evening after he told her good night, but she told him to come join them whenever he felt up to it.

"I'll be there in time for dinner," he said, giving her a brief kiss.

"Okay," she said, stepping away and joining the others who were heading for the camping area beyond the gentle dunes lining the edge of the sandy beach.

Everyone gathered in the open area of their campsite between the two groups of tents, and Isaac wanted them all to share things they remembered about the summer: significant moments they'd had in their journey with God or they had guided their campers in. Mandy thought of several things she could share, but her mind kept wandering to Matt, and every time someone else finished sharing and she realized they had stopped talking, another person had already started.

She was worried about him. She could understand him wanting time alone, but she wasn't sure he had been completely honest. At four-thirty she couldn't wait any longer and quietly left the group. She needed to check on him and make sure he was okay.

Heading toward the sound of the ocean, she came over the top of the dune, scanned the beach, and saw him sitting where she had left him thirty minutes ago.

The closer she got, the more concerned she became. He was sitting like she had found him last Sunday in Mark's room: elbows on his knees, head in his hands, still and silent.

He didn't hear her coming and twitched when she touched him. She fell on her knees beside him. He looked up, and she could see he had been crying. She didn't apologize for her intrusion, and she was willing to leave him alone if that's what he wanted, but he was going to have to convince her of that.

"I was worried about you," she said. "Are you okay?"

He didn't say anything. He didn't look good at all.

"You can talk to me, Matthew. Whatever it is. If you want me to leave you alone, I will. But I'm here. You don't have to shut me out."

He took a deep breath and let out a tension-filled sigh. "You're not going to like it," he said. "I don't like it."

"What?"

He didn't say it right away, but she waited. And by the time he spoke, she had already thought of what it might be. "I'm thinking of not going to college right now, at least not to Lifegate. I think I should stay here with my family."

She had her response ready. "If that's what you decide, Matthew, it's fine with me."

He didn't want to accept her words. "Amanda, we've been waiting four months to start seeing each other every day."

"I know."

"So, what? You're not going to miss me?"

"No, I'm not."

The look on his face was priceless, and she smiled. "If you stay, I'll stay."

"You'll stay? What about your scholarship?"

"It's a private scholarship. I can use it wherever I want."

He stared at her. "I won't let you do that, Amanda."

"Oh, really? And what makes you the boss of me?"

"Amanda, your parents would never forgive me for getting in the way of your dreams. I would never forgive myself."

She reached into her back pocket and pulled out an envelope. She had been waiting for the right moment to show him the letter she had written to him last Saturday night but had never mailed. She'd completely forgotten about it until she had seen the addressed envelope on the shelf beside her bed this morning.

She handed it to him and asked him to read it. She couldn't remember exactly what she had said, but she knew it had something about her not being sure about going off to college and feeling indecisive about what she wanted to study.

"When did you write this?" he asked after he finished.

"Last Saturday. I never mailed it because the next day I was in Portland with you."

"Why didn't you say something?"

"I forgot about it until I saw it in my cabin this morning, and then when I remembered what I had written, I knew immediately if you decided you didn't want to go to school right now, I shouldn't either."

"You knew I was thinking that?"

"I thought you might be."

"And you're okay with it?"

"Lifegate isn't my dream. It's an opportunity that seemed like the best option at the time. And maybe we'll end up there eventually. But it doesn't matter to me. You matter, Matthew. I want to be with you, wherever that is."

He didn't say anything, and she decided to tease him. "Unless, of course, you're tired of me and are looking for a good reason to put some distance between us."

He smiled. "Well, this *is* the eighth day in a row I've seen you."

"I know! And who knows when that's going to end? I could be bugging you every single day for the next—whatever."

He kissed her tenderly and pulled her onto his lap, holding her gently in his arms. "For the rest of my life, Amanda."

She draped her arms around his neck and allowed him to kiss her the way he wanted to. He was so gentle with her, so tenderly possessive. The rest of the world was forgotten, and she didn't care about anything except sharing her life with this incredibly special person.

Her life made sense with Matthew. Her uncertainties about the future and her insecurities about herself melted away. She had no idea what they would be doing a month from now, but if they were together, that was enough. That was all she needed to know.

And she knew they would be. A summer of week-long separations hadn't driven them apart. His brother's death hadn't made him push her away. His parents' lack of acceptance of her had brought them closer. And a major change in their college plans only made her feel more excited about how God would lead them.

"Is there anything else you want to talk about, Matthew? You can tell me anything. Don't keep things inside."

"There is something," he said. "Something I want to ask you."

She waited for him to continue.

"Could you honestly marry someone like me, Amanda?"

She smiled. "I don't know about someone *like* you, but I know I could marry you."

"Why on earth would you want to do a crazy thing like that?"

She laughed. "I don't know what you see when you look in the mirror, Matthew, but I see someone completely wonderful. Kind and sweet, gentle and loving. Someone with a pure heart. Someone who loves God and others. Someone who has learned from his mistakes. Someone who lost his brother tragically this week and yet is so concerned about how that affects me? I'm in love with you for a reason, Matthew, not just because you're cute and you asked me out."

"Why do you have so much faith in me?"

"Because you've never given me any reason to not have faith in you. When I see you, I see you for who you are now, not for who you've been in the past."

He pulled her close to him. "I hope I never let you down, Amanda."

"Just love me and be who you are, Matthew. That's all I need."

He started crying softly, as he had often this week, but she knew these tears were coming from a different place in his heart. Not a place of despair and grief, but of hope and joy.

"That's all I need too, baby," he said. "Just love me and let me love you. That's all I want."

Chapter Twenty-Five

Hiking the final stretch of the trail leading out of the Silver Creek Canyon, Lauren didn't want to leave. She was getting hungry and thought Adam's suggestion of heading back to civilization and getting pizza for dinner sounded good, but it had been a perfect day. Perfect weather. Perfect setting. Perfect company. Perfect conversation. And some very perfect kissing. She felt amazed by how close she already felt to Adam. Physically, emotionally, and spiritually. She could tell him anything and had done so today, even more than last weekend and in her notes and brief encounters with him throughout the week.

She had appreciated the honest conversation Adam had initiated about having standards and boundaries concerning where they spent time alone together in the future and what they would and wouldn't do during that time. Adam had strong personal beliefs about what forms of physical affection were acceptable and what were not. She hadn't disagreed with anything he had said, and while two weeks ago she wouldn't have thought some of it needed to be mentioned, today she had been more aware of how easy it could be to compromise and do things she never would imagine herself or any decent Christian guy doing before marriage.

Personal ideals were one thing. Before she had kissed Adam down by the river last Saturday, she had seen the idea of sexual purity as a black and white issue. Hand-holding, hugging, kissing—these things were fine. Making out, touching private areas, having sex—those things weren't. It seemed simple, obvious, a no-brainer. But that was before Adam had kissed her lips so sweetly and made her feel so desirable to him. Now it seemed complicated, not so easy to control, and something she could easily justify as "anything-goes" as long as they both agreed to it.

Adam said he felt the same way since kissing her last weekend, and that's why he knew they needed to talk about it. And his genuine desire to treat her respectfully and guard their relationship had been evident today. She knew the potential for mistakes was there, but she also felt safe and confident in Adam's ability to guard their time.

"Did you have a nice time today?" Adam asked.

"Yes, I don't want to leave."

He smiled. "We don't have to."

"No, I am getting hungry, and those mosquitoes were starting to bug me," she said. "But I did have a nice time with you. It's been a perfect day."

"What was your favorite part?"

"I liked sitting with you on that rock."

"The kissing or the talking?"

"Both. I appreciated everything you said, especially about praying for each other and letting me know you want me to go to Blake or Seth if I want them to talk to you about how we're spending our time together."

"Did I do anything today that made you uncomfortable, even a little?"

"No," she replied honestly. "But your kisses have a powerful effect on me. I wasn't expecting that. Last weekend I thought it was the newness of it, but—"

She felt embarrassed at her admission, but Adam took it seriously. Pulling her close to him, he held her and whispered, "I never want to cause us to stumble, Angel. I'll be careful. I promise."

She believed him and lifted her face to look into his caring blue eyes. He seemed too good to be true, but she knew he was exactly what she had been praying for.

"May I kiss you now, or have you had enough for today?" he asked.

"You may," she said.

He kissed her in a similar way as he had been all day, and she melted into his sweet affection. Adam's kisses seemed to have one speed: passionate.

"You know what my favorite part of the day was?" he said.

"What?"

"Just now when you were completely honest with me about how I make you feel. You make me feel that way too. That's why I wanted to talk about it. Your kisses—everything about you has a powerful effect on me. A dangerous effect, Angel."

His words surprised her. She wasn't some beauty queen. She didn't have a body guys stared at. She wasn't a Kerri or a Jessica. What exactly did Adam see in her? She still wasn't clear on that.

"Why, Adam?"

"Why?"

"Yes. Why do I affect you like that?"

"Because you're beautiful," he said like there was no arguing that point. "Ever since God hit me with a two-by-four and opened my eyes to see you, I haven't been able to look away. I don't see other girls anymore, Lauren. I just see you."

"Not even Kerri?" she asked seriously.

"Not even Kerri. I don't know what you've done to me, Angel, but you've definitely done something, and I'm not certain because I've never been there before, but I think I'm falling in love with you."

She smiled and cherished the thought. She wasn't certain either because she had never been in love, but she felt the same way and dared to tell him so.

"I think I'm falling in love with you too. And if I'm not, I'm going to be in serious trouble when I do."

***

With the late afternoon sun hanging above the shimmering Pacific Ocean, Seth stepped behind Amber and slipped his arms around her waist, laid his chin on her shoulder, and whispered in her ear.

"What are you thinking about?"

She kept looking at the ocean waves and replied. "All of the ways our friends have been touched by our relationship."

He had thought that several times today too. He had thought about it most when Matt had shared at Fireside last night, remembering the times Matt had been one of the kids sitting on those benches listening to others talk about the difference God had made in their life, and how often he had prayed Matt would listen; and now he was the one up there preaching it. It had brought tears to his eyes and made him cry outright when he talked to his guys about it before bed. He'd had good guys this week and had said, 'If you have things in your life that need fixing, ask God to fix them, and if you have friends who are in trouble, don't stop praying for them because God has you in their life for a reason.'

"It's great to be a part of what God is doing, isn't it?" he said, wondering what else God would be doing in their lives and those around them in the future.

"Yes," she said, turning to face him. "And it's great to be a part of it with you."

He kissed her and made it last. They had one more week until he would be able to hold her and kiss her anytime, anywhere once again. And he was looking forward to it.

"I love you, Amber. This was a tough week for me, but seeing you every morning and all of your little notes helped me to keep going."

"I'm glad," she said. "It's not often I feel like you need me."

"I need you, Amber. All the time. It might not seem like it, but that's only because you don't see me without you. My life would be very different. I would be very different."

"And you know who you would be dating?"

"Who?"

"If you had gone to camp this summer without a girlfriend, and I wasn't there, you would be dating Lauren right now."

"What makes you think that?"

"You don't?"

"I didn't say that."

She laughed. "Oh, so you agree, do you?"

"She's a lot like you."

"Perfect for Adam."

"Whom you would be dating if I hadn't met you first."

"He's even cuter than he was last summer."

Seth put his hand over his chest, faking a heart attack. "Oh, baby. Don't do that to me."

She laughed and gave him a sweet kiss. "But you're still cuter," she said, scrunching up her nose in that cute way he loved so much.

He kissed her back. "I think God knew what He was doing when He had us meet each other first."

"I think so too," she said, kissing him in a dangerous way. He knew she didn't realize it, and she had only begun kissing him that way recently. He wasn't sure what it was, but it made him feel things in a hurry.

"You can't kiss me like that," he said, stepping back to let her know he was serious.

"Like what?"

"The way you were kissing me. I don't know what you're doing there, but you can't."

"You're serious?"

"Yes, Amber. I'm very serious."

"Okay," she said. "I'm sorry."

"It's okay. Just no more."

She smiled at him and leaned into his chest, letting out a sigh and wrapping her arms around his waist. "I love being engaged to you, Seth. I love the way it makes me feel."

"How does it make you feel?"

"Safe and protected and loved—but in a different way than before."

"I like being engaged to you too. It makes me feel like I'm taking care of you, and I like that feeling."

"Let's not break up, okay?"

He laughed. "Okay."

She lifted her head from his shoulder and looked up at him. He kissed her in a way he could handle right now, and she simply accepted it.

"I love you, sweetheart. I always have, and I always will."

"I love you too, Seth. Always and forever."

"This shirt looks nice on you." He had always thought she looked great in red, and he had found the perfect t-shirt for her this afternoon. On the front it had sailboats, and on the back it said, "Drifting my way?" It reminded him of her ability to lead people in the right direction—toward God mostly—and she didn't do much except seek after God herself, and others seemed to follow.

He had shared why he bought it for her earlier, and he commented on one specific way she had influenced someone. She had never said a word to Matt about the bad choices he was making, but she'd had a huge impact on him just the same.

"You know Matt is where he is today largely because of you, don't you?"

She appeared perplexed. "You mean you."

"No. I mean you. I told him the same things over and over, but it wasn't until the night of the dance last winter he finally listened, and he did because he knew he wanted a girl like you, and I said, 'You're never going to get a girl like that unless you change your ways.'"

She smiled. "But he had you as an example to follow."

"And you were the one who prayed for a good girl for him. I didn't have the faith to pray for that yet. I thought he needed to be heading in the right direction for a year or more before he would be ready for another relationship, not three months, and I know you were a huge part of getting Mandy to have enough confidence in herself to believe it could happen."

"Me and Jesus," she said. "I told her things, but it was Jesus who gave me the right words. My initial advice was way off-base. I told her she needed to change, but then I heard that God saying, 'Nope. That's not right, Amber. Mandy can be exactly who I have made her to be, and Matt will be drawn to her quietness and gentle spirit.'"

"Are you still working on that story about them?"

"Yes, and after this week, I think I know how it's going to end, I just need time to write it."

"Have you thought more about taking a lighter class-load this semester so you'll have time to write?"

"I think I'm going to. This week I had a girl in my cabin who has quite the story, and I already have it started in my head."

"Matt told me he might not be going to school right away. How do you think Mandy will handle that?"

"She'll stay here too."

"How do you know?"

"She told me."

"But Matt said he hadn't talked to her about it yet. He asked me to pray for him to have the courage to be honest with her today."

Amber smiled. "If Matt doesn't think Mandy has thought of that possibility, he's got another thing coming. She asked me to pray he would do what God is leading him to do."

"And she's fine with them staying here?"

"That's what she told me."

"Maybe we should pray for them now."

Seth took her hands and prayed for Matt and Mandy and also for themselves, asking God to lead them as they finished out the summer and headed off into the great unknown of college life in another two weeks. He was looking forward to it and felt scared at the same time. He was happy about being engaged to Amber and knew marrying her next summer was the right choice for them, but he also felt the added responsibility of being in a position to take care of her and figure out his future.

Sometimes when they prayed together, Amber would let him pray and she wouldn't add anything, but today she did at the end of his rambling that felt more like a meeting with his career counselor than his God. Her words calmed him and reminded him of the truth.

"Jesus, we're just a couple of your children feeling a little scared about the future. We know we shouldn't because you already have it all taken care of, and we just need to follow where You lead us. You've shown us that over and over, and we ask for faith to believe that. May we trust you, Jesus. May we trust you with all the details.

"You are our God, and we love you. Give us peace. We're going to a new place with new challenges and without our parents to always turn to, but we know you remain the same. May we taste and see your goodness like we have here. We want to know you. We want to see you. We want to walk in the paths You have for us. May we do that, Jesus. With your help and love, may we do that."

Seth opened his eyes and stared at her. So beautiful. So honest. So calm. So much of what he needed. He meant it when he said his life would be so different without her. She could boost his faith with a few simple words or a heartfelt prayer as much as his youth pastor or other dynamic speakers. She lived the truth of God like no one he had ever met, and she was his fiancée—the person he was going to spend the rest of his life with and have by his side through whatever they faced.

Closing his eyes, he found her lips and kissed her, feeling like he never wanted to stop. And it wasn't the physical pleasure of it that fueled his desire, it was her. Her spirit and her life. Her closeness and her support. Her peace and her joy. Her companionship. Her love.

Chapter Twenty-Six

Lauren enjoyed the feeling of Adam's soft lips as twilight surrounded them. After having dinner at the same pizza place where they had eaten last Saturday, Adam had brought her to the park by the river again, and she had enjoyed the past hour they had been sitting here talking and kissing and enjoying perfect moments together that seemed to be defining their relationship so far.

Adam's kisses were amazing. They made her feel special and beautiful and gave her nice feelings she had never experienced before, but they were also controlled and non-threatening. She didn't feel the need to stop him or push him away. She didn't feel he was trying to take them down a path they shouldn't be on. His affection was passionate but innocent. Sensuous but pure. Kisses of affection and love, not lust and uncontrolled desire.

"I take back what I said earlier. I'm definitely falling in love with you, Angel. I'm not sure how that's possible this soon, but it's happening. I can't stop myself."

Questions of 'Why me?' entered her mind. She believed what he was saying, but she wondered why he was saying it. "What exactly do you like about me?"

"I like everything about you, Lauren. You're fun to be with, and you're easy to talk to. You're kind and sweet and unselfish. You're close to God. You listen to me, and you're honest and real. You're like some of the really good friends I've had who I instantly got along with and enjoyed spending time with, but you're a girl. A very beautiful girl I love to kiss and hold in my arms and make you smile."

"You're good at that," she said, smiling at him once again.

"What do you like about me?"

"Besides the kissing?"

He smiled. "Yes, besides that."

She thought for a moment, wanting to answer as honestly as possible. It was a lot of things, she realized, and she said them all.

"You're caring and honest. You make me laugh. You're fun to be with and easy to talk to. When I'm with you, I feel like you want to be with me, not like you would just as well be somewhere else. You make me feel special. You're more than I ever hoped to dream for. I've prayed for a guy like you, but I wasn't sure if any existed or if one of them would ever notice me."

"But you're the kind of girl we're looking for," he said. "Us good guys who want a real relationship, not just a good time. I love talking to you. I feel comfortable with you, not like I'm trying to impress you or get you to like me. You don't make me work for it. You like me for who I am."

"And you like me for who I am," she said, realizing that also. She hadn't thought about it before, but she knew Adam wasn't making her work for it either. She was simply being herself, and he liked her. He wanted her, not someone she had to pretend to be.

"Yes, Angel," he said, stroking her cheek and running his fingers into her hair. "I do. When I see you, I like what I see. Inside and out. You don't have to be anyone but yourself. That's who I want. That's who I'm kissing."

He kissed her one last time and then kept his word about not keeping her here too late. When they arrived at the camp, he walked her from the parking area to the girls' cabins, and he handed her a note he had written last night before bed.

"If today went like I hoped, I knew saying these things would be appropriate, but if you gave me any indication you didn't want this, I didn't want to put any pressure on you. I'm just sharing my heart, Angel. I hope it doesn't scare you too much."

"If you hear a really loud scream coming from this way, then you'll know."

He laughed and gave her a hug. "Meet me before breakfast in the morning?" he asked.

"Sure. What time?"

"Eight-thirty?"

"I'll be there," she said, stepping back and giving him one last smile. "Thanks for the great day."

***

When Amber and Seth returned to camp with the rest of their group, it was only nine-thirty, and they spent another hour talking by the lake. Amber didn't want to stay up too late. She'd had a fun but tiring week, and with middle school girls coming, she knew she needed to get some good sleep tonight. She loved junior high girls the most, but they had endless energy, and at this point in the summer, her energy level had been depleted.

Seth walked her to the trail leading to the girls' cabins and said good-night to her there, giving her a long hug and telling her he loved her, something she never got tired of hearing. She had enjoyed their day together and was looking forward to next weekend, but she had one week left, and she planned to give it her all.

She decided to take a shower before bed so she wouldn't have to get up as early in the morning. The warm water felt nice, and she didn't rush. After she dried herself off and got dressed, she stepped out to the sink area and saw Lauren brushing her teeth. She hadn't gotten to know Lauren well this summer because her cabin was at the other end of the girls' cabin area and she usually spent Saturdays with Seth while Lauren had spent time hanging around with Kerri. But she really liked her and believed what she had told Seth about him going for a girl like that. She hadn't thought about her and Adam getting together, mainly because she knew Adam liked Kerri, but now that it was happening, she could see they were perfect for each other.

"Hi, Lauren," she said. "How was your day?"

"Nice," Lauren said.

"I heard Adam took you to Silver Falls. I love that place."

Lauren finished with her teeth and rinsed her mouth out with water before responding. "Me too. I've only been there once before, and I never imagined I would be going there on a date."

"Or that your date would be Adam?"

Lauren smiled. "No, definitely not. I have no idea why this is happening."

"I felt the same way about Seth when we first started dating."

"You did?"

"Yes, are you kidding? Me, with a guy like that? For about a month I was convinced it was just a dream and I was going to wake up any second."

"I know. I can't believe we're going to the same college and everything. For so long I thought I was never going to have a boyfriend, and now he's here, and it's so perfect. No wonder God didn't want me dating anyone else."

"Speaking of college," Amber said. "Are you rooming with anyone you know, or did you ask for a random assignment?"

"Random," she said. "I didn't know anyone else who was going there until this summer."

"I might be looking for a new roommate. Are you interested?"

"What about your cousin?"

"She and Matt might not be going. With the accident and everything, Matt feels like he should stay here, and if he stays, Mandy is staying too. I should know by this week sometime."

"Yeah, I'd love to room with you if that's possible. You're with Kerri and Jess too, right?"

"Yep. We'd love to have you if it works out."

"Okay, thanks. Let me know."

"I will," Amber said, plugging in her blow-dryer so she could dry her hair before going out into the cool night air. Lauren was finished and told her good-night before leaving.

"Good night, Lauren. Sweet dreams."

Lauren smiled. "I'm sure they will be."

Amber dried her hair and then returned to her cabin. Before she turned out her light, she took her journal and wrote out prayers about things that were heavy on her mind. For Lauren and Adam, Mandy and Matt, and for Seth. He'd been more tense and worried about the future than she had seen before, and she knew that wasn't how it should be. She felt that way from time to time too, but right now she had complete confidence God was going to lead them like He always had and they needed to trust Him and enjoy the ride.

She had tucked the poem she had written for Seth several months ago inside her journal after giving Colleen a copy of it yesterday. Unfolding it and reading the words once again, she suddenly saw the words with different eyes, and she wrote out a new poem that was similar but talked about the way she saw God.

When I see You, Jesus
I see who I could be
If I believe
and trust You in everything

When I see You, Jesus
I forget what lies behind

And I press on to what lies ahead
To the perfect plans You have for me

When I see You, Jesus
I see Love in all its glory
Reaching out to me
Your child in need

When I see You, Jesus
I see the joy and peace
You offer me
When I let You reign

She heard God respond, and she wrote the words
He spoke to her:

When I see you, Amber
I don't see who you've been
But who you can be
With Me

When I see you, Amber
I don't see the mistakes
And the missteps you've taken
I see where we can go from here

When I see you, Amber
I see what happens
When Love has entered your heart
And let it reign anew

When I see you, Amber
I see you as we
are meant to be
—Together

Thank you for another great summer, Jesus. For all the work You've done in my heart and those who have come through my cabin door. I pray for those who were here this week, especially Destiny. May she know you for who you really are instead of the way she's seen you for so long. May she and all of the girls I've had this summer understand how much you love them.

I pray for Adam and Lauren also, that they could have a relationship like Seth and I have. May it be all about loving you together and loving each other with a pure, unselfish love that grows and thrives in the coming months. I pray this also for Matt and Mandy, Blake and Colleen, Jessica and Chad, Stacey and Kenny, Hope and Ben, and me and Seth. Show us your ways, Jesus. Lead us in your truth and teach us. Be our God and help us to trust you. May we walk with you, run with you, dance with you, and climb with you to the high places.

I pray these things also for Kerri and for whomever that special guy is you have waiting for her. I trust you to bring them together at the right time and help them to wait with patience, hope, and peace. Draw them both closer to you and teach them whatever they need to learn before they meet each other and begin the journey you have for them together.

I already prayed for this, but I want to write out my request that you would help Seth to trust you as he seeks the path You have for him as a college student, as someone who has a strong desire to be a part of your kingdom work, and as my fiancé. I know it's a lot for him to carry. Help him to remember he doesn't have to figure it out all by himself—that you are there and will be faithful to lead him one day at a time.

Chapter Twenty-Seven

Before going to her cabin, Lauren decided to see if Kerri was in. She hadn't been earlier, but seeing Amber down at the bathroom, Lauren knew they were back from the beach.

"Hey, you are here," she said when Kerri opened the door.

"I am," she said. "And so are you."

Lauren laughed and stepped into the cabin, giving Kerri a hug and responding to her words. "We both decided we needed to get back a little earlier tonight. Adam has Blake to answer to this time, and I need more sleep than I got last Saturday."

"How was it?" Kerri asked, sitting on her bed and leaving room for her to join her.

Lauren sat down and leaned against the wall. "It was very nice. Perfect."

"Wow," Kerri said. "Perfect? Really?"

"Really. It was fun, it was romantic, it was serious, it was relaxed, it was real, it was magical. Perfect."

Kerri smiled. "I'm glad. I'm truly happy for you."

"How was your day?"

"Fine," she said. "Sort of weird, I guess. I've spent this whole summer being single and yet having

Dylan at the same time. Today it was back to being just me, but it gave me a lot of time to think. It was good."

"I saw Amber down at the bathroom. She said her cousin might not be going to Lifegate, and she asked if I wanted to room with her if she doesn't."

"I didn't know Mandy wasn't going."

"It's not for sure. She's going to let me know."

"That would be perfect," Kerri said. "Then I can really keep an eye on Adam."

Lauren laughed, knowing that wasn't the only reason Kerri would be happy to have her in the adjoining room of the suite-like dorms. "I hope it works out. I thought it was great the three of you already knew each other, but I was a little jealous."

"Do you have any details to share about today, possible new roommate, or would you rather keep it all to yourself?"

Lauren felt free to share the majority of it, and she did. She told Kerri about the honest conversation they'd had about boundaries and spending their time together wisely, and she also told her how challenging she knew it would be to stick with the plan.

"It's not Adam who's making me feel that way, it's just me. I mean it's him," she laughed, "but he's just kissing me. It's my own thoughts going places they've never been before. Pray for me—a lot!"

"I will," she said. "And anytime you need to talk, I'm here, okay?"

"I know," she said, sitting forward and giving her a hug. "Thanks, Kerri."

She rose from the bed. If she didn't, she would end up sitting here talking to *Kerri* until midnight. Kerri walked her to the door, and she stepped outside.

"Lauren?"

She turned back. "Yeah?"

"With the exception of my brother, you're the best friend I've ever had."

Lauren was stunned. "I am?"

"Yes. I was thinking about that today when you weren't there. I'm glad about where you were instead, but I missed you."

"You know something funny?"

"What?"

"Last Saturday when you were gone, I was completely bored by lunchtime, and I realized how close we had become. I remember praying on the way up to the staff lounge things would go well between you and Dylan, but I was also thinking about how glad I was you had a boyfriend who wasn't here because otherwise we might not have become good friends. And I didn't think about it until just now, but Dylan not only contributed to us becoming friends, but also to me ending up here alone with Adam last weekend."

Kerri laughed. "Maybe you should send him a thank-you note."

"Maybe I will," she laughed in return. "But for now I'll say thanks to you for being a great friend to me too."

"Good night," Kerri said. "Sleep well."

"I think I will," she said. "See you tomorrow."

Returning to her cabin, Lauren felt stunned by the way Kerri saw her, but she was happy to accept it as a reality. She saw Kerri as someone who had tons of friends and didn't need the friendship of someone she had met this summer and happened to be assigned to the cabin next door. Kerri was pretty and popular, and Lauren usually felt intimidated and inferior to girls like her. But she had never felt that way with Kerri.

Lauren recalled one of her greatest prayers of this past school year. Almost from the beginning of her senior year she had felt strongly led to work at camp this summer and to attend Lifegate this fall, and she had prayed at least one of her friends from either church or school would end up doing the same. She had lived in the same town all her life and gone to the same church and the same schools with her friends, and the thought of leaving all of that had been scary. She had been hoping for one friend to make the transition with her, but it hadn't happened, and she began the summer feeling abandoned by God—like He couldn't fulfill that one small request.

But then she met Kerri and other girls here and was able to be more herself with them than those she had known for years back home. She was able to see her prayers may not have been answered in the exact way she had hoped for, but God had answered. No one from back home was going to Lifegate with her, but three girls she had met here this summer were, and she might end up being roommates with them. She was going to be heading off to college with a sweet boyfriend too. This week they had been reminded life could change quickly with unexpected tragedy. But her own life had been turned upside-down in a pleasant way.

Once she had changed into her pajamas and gotten into bed, Lauren took the note Adam had given her and unfolded it. By what he said when he gave it to her, she expected it to be serious. The thought of dating had often scared her in the past, but she couldn't feel more at peace about it now. She didn't see Adam as some guy she was dating. She saw him as the best friend she'd ever had.

Dear Lauren,

Have you ever had a moment where you felt like God was so close you could touch Him? Have you ever prayed for something for months on end, and just when you had given up hope of it ever happening, there it was? Have you ever seen God answer in a way you didn't expect, but when the answer came you couldn't imagine it being more perfect?

I have. Last Saturday was like that for me. I woke up thinking it was going to be the worst day of the summer, and it ended up being the best. So far, anyway. I'm writing this on Thursday, and I have a feeling this Saturday is going to be even better. If it's not, then maybe this isn't what I think it is, and you probably won't be reading this letter. So if you are, then everything I'm about to say is still true, and it's so strong I'm almost afraid to say it because I don't want to get ahead of God, but at the same time I can't not say it. I've never felt this way before about anyone or felt so certain of anything in my life.

You're the girl I've spent the last two years praying for, Angel. The girl I asked God to have wait for me and I promised to wait for. I've tried to put other girls in that place, but this time I know it's not me that's doing it, it's God. When He opened my eyes to see you, it was like a lightning bolt and a gentle whisper; like a crashing ocean wave and the rising sun; like nothing I'd ever imagined and something so familiar I barely gave it a second thought.

Kissing you makes my heart beat differently. It makes me forget about time and space. Even the thought of it now makes my lips tingle and my soul long for you. Like you're the piece that's been missing without me realizing it, but now that I've found you, it aches to not have you there. I'm scared, Angel. I'm scared of spending Saturday with you and having it not be like that anymore. Of discovering Saturday was just a dream, a point in time that seemed so perfect, but then vanishes into thin air.

If you're reading this, that didn't happen for me, and I hope it didn't for you either. I don't want this unless you do. Don't fake anything for me, Angel. I know I'm the first guy you've dated, and maybe in a few weeks or months your feelings for me will fade. I don't expect you to base any future decisions on what has happened between us this summer. But I want you to know I will be very surprised if any of this goes away for me. I'm not a spontaneous person. I tend to pray and think about things for months—Kerri is a perfect example of that. But with you, I couldn't. At first I was thinking,

'Okay, Adam. Take some time. Pray about this before you kiss her. Wait until next weekend, maybe longer. Don't do something on a whim.' But then I remembered all those times I'd prayed before, and I heard God whisper, 'This is it, Adam. This is her, the one you've been waiting for. And you don't have to wait another second.'

I've been feeling a little lost about going to college. I'm not sure what I want to study. I don't feel God leading me in any particular direction, but suddenly that seems so secondary. Whatever paths God takes us on from here, I just hope they're side-by-side and eventually will merge into one.

With all my heart,
Adam

Blessed are the pure in heart,
for they will see God.
Matthew 5:8

In the morning Lauren got up earlier than she usually did on Sundays, took a shower and got dressed, and then headed up to the lake. Adam wouldn't be arriving for another half-hour, but she had gotten up early on purpose. She spent those extra minutes writing a letter to him she had been too tired to write last night, and the words flowed easily. She felt like Adam did about being almost afraid to write it out, but at the same time she couldn't not write it.

By the time she heard Adam's footsteps approaching her on the path, she had finished the letter and was sitting there on the bench with her eyes closed. He sat down and whispered, "What are you doing way over here?"

She opened her eyes and smiled. Normally they met on one of the benches closer to the other end of the lake, but she had chosen this more distant one deliberately.

"I thought we would be less likely to get caught kissing."

He laughed. "I hope you're serious."

She considered it for a brief moment. Nobody was around, but she decided it wouldn't be a good idea. Just yesterday she had told herself she would never tempt Adam to do something he shouldn't. It was just a kiss, but that wasn't allowed, so she told him the real reason she had wanted to sit here this morning.

"Actually, I sat here because of something you wrote in your letter."

"You read it?"

"Yes. Didn't you hear me scream?"

He laughed. "Uh-oh."

"No, I didn't," she said. "I wasn't shocked by anything you said. I mean, I was because you're you and I'm me, but it's not like you didn't tell me most of it yesterday."

"What do you mean, 'I'm me and you're you'?"

"You know what I mean, Adam. I'm trying not to feel that way, but it's going to take me awhile to believe this is actually happening."

He leaned over and kissed her cheek. "It is, Angel."

"I know."

"So, what about the letter made you sit here?" he asked, getting back to the original topic.

"The part where you talked about praying for the last two years for me. I'd forgotten something until I read that. I've been praying for you too, but I forgot where that started."

"Where?"

"Right here."

"As in, right here on this bench?"

"Yes."

"When?"

"Two years ago. I came here for a week as a camper, and Tamara was my counselor. She told us about the guy she had started dating a few months before and how she had been praying for him for a long time. One afternoon that week, I think it was Thursday, I was feeling depressed because I was sixteen and I'd never been on a date or been kissed, and I remembered what Tamara had said, so I sat down on this bench and I prayed for the right guy at the right time and for the patience to wait for him."

He smiled. "I was working here that summer."

"I know!" She laughed. "Isn't that wild?"

"Did you know Blake was my counselor the summer before?"

"No."

"Yep. He was the one who encouraged me to apply to be on staff."

Lauren looked up at the sky. It was a brilliant blue this morning, and she knew it would turn into a hot August day, but for now it was beautiful and refreshing, like her life and her heart.

"Blessed are the pure in heart," Adam whispered, *"for they will see God."*

Lauren felt tingly all over. Her God had done this for her, and not just this summer. He had been planning it and pulling all the pieces together for a long time.

Yes, Jesus. I see You. It's been cloudy for awhile, but you've broken through the clouds like you promised. Thank you. You are forever faithful.

*I'd love to hear how God has used
this story to touch your heart.*

Write me at:

living_loved@yahoo.com

Additional Titles in the Pure in Heart Series

When I'm With You

When I Trust You

When I'm Loving You

Made in the USA
Middletown, DE
03 June 2020